I0749292

The Inside Of The Cup

Volume 5

Winston Churchill

The Inside Of The Cup, Vol 5.

Winston Churchill

PO Box 2211
Fairfield, IA 52556
www.1stworldlibrary.org
First Edition

LCCN: 2003099817

Softcover ISBN: 1-59540-143-1
Hardcover ISBN: 1-4218-0693-2
eBook ISBN: 1-59540-193-8

Purchase *"The Inside Of The Cup, Vol 5."*
as a traditional bound book at:
www.1stWorldLibrary.org/purchase.asp?ISBN=1-59540-143-1

1st World Library Literary Society is a nonprofit organization dedicated to promoting literacy by:

- Creating a free internet library accessible from any computer worldwide.
- Hosting writing competitions and offering book publishing scholarships.

The Inside Of The Cup, Vol 5.

contributed by Ed ,Tim & Rodney
in support of
1st World Library Literary Society

TABLE OF CONTENTS

Volume 5

CHAPTER XVII

RECONSTRUCTION

I

Life had indeed become complicated, paradoxical. He, John Hodder, a clergyman, rector of St. John's by virtue of not having resigned, had entered a restaurant of ill repute, had ordered champagne for an abandoned woman, and had no sense of sin when he awoke the next morning! The devil, in the language of orthodox theology, had led him there. He had fallen under the influence of the tempter of his youth, and all in him save the carnal had been blotted out.

More paradoxes! If the devil had not taken possession of him and led him there, it were more than probable that he could never have succeeded in any other way in getting on a footing of friendship with this woman, Kate Marcy. Her future, to be sure, was problematical. Here was no simple, sentimental case he might formerly have imagined, of trusting innocence betrayed, but a mixture of good and evil, selfishness and unselfishness. And she had, in spite of all, known the love which effaces self!. Could the disintegration, in her case, be arrested?

Gradually Hodder was filled with a feeling which may

be called amazement because, although his brain was no nearer to a solution than before, he was not despondent. For a month he had not permitted his mind to dwell on the riddle; yet this morning he felt stirring within him a new energy for which he could not account, a hope unconnected with any mental process! He felt in touch, once more, faintly but perceptibly, with something stable in the chaos. In bygone years he had not seen the chaos, but the illusion of an orderly world, a continual succession of sunrises, 'couleur de rose', from the heights above Bremerton. Now were the scales fallen from his eyes; now he saw the evil, the injustice, the despair; felt, in truth, the weight of the sorrow of it all, and yet that sorrow was unaccountably transmuted, as by a chemical process, into something which for the first time had a meaning - he could not say what meaning. The sting of despair had somehow been taken out of it, and it remained poignant!

Not on the obsession of the night before, when he had walked down Dalton Street and beheld it transformed into a realm of adventure, but upon his past life did he look back now with horror, upon the even tenor of those days and years in the bright places. His had been the highroad of a fancied security, from which he had feared to stray, to seek his God across the rough face of nature, from black, forgotten capons to the flying peaks in space. He had feared reality. He had insisted upon gazing at the universe through the coloured glasses of an outworn theology, instead of using his own eyes.

So he had left the highroad, the beaten way of salvation many others had deserted, had flung off his spectacles, had plunged into reality, to be scratched and battered, to lose his way. Not until now had something of grim zest come to him, of an instinct which was the first groping of a vision, as to where his own path might lie. Through what thickets and over what mountains he knew not as yet - nor cared to know. He felt resistance, whereas on the highroad he had felt none. On the highroad his cry had gone unheeded and unheard, yet by holding out his hand in the wilderness he had helped another, bruised and bleeding, to her feet! Salvation, Let it be what it might be, he would go on, stumbling and seeking, through reality.

Even this last revelation, of Eldon Parr's agency in another tragedy, seemed to have no further power to affect him. . . Nor could Hodder think of Alison as in blood-relationship to the financier, or even to the boy, whose open, pleasure-loving face he had seen in the photograph.

II

A presage of autumn was in the air, and a fine, misty rain drifted in at his windows as he sat at his breakfast. He took deep breaths of the moisture, and it seemed to water and revive his parching soul. He found himself, to his surprise, surveying with equanimity the pile of books in the corner which had led him to the conviction of the emptiness of the universe - but the universe was no longer empty! It was cruel, but a warring force was at work in it which was not blind, but directed. He could not say why this was so, but he knew it, he felt it, sensed its energy within him as he set out for Dalton Street.

He was neither happy nor unhappy, but in equilibrium, walking with sure steps, and the anxiety in which he had fallen asleep the night before was gone: anxiety lest the woman should have fled, or changed her mind, or committed some act of desperation.

In Dalton Street a thin coat of yellow mud glistened on the asphalt, but even the dreariness of this neighbourhood seemed transient. He rang the bell of the flat, the door swung open, and in the hall above a woman awaited him. She was clad in black.

"You wouldn't know me, would you?" she inquired. "Say, I scarcely know myself. I used to wear this dress at Pratt's, with white collars and cuffs and - well, I just put it on again. I had it in the bottom of my trunk, and I guessed you'd like it."

"I didn't know you at first," he said, and the pleasure in

his face was her reward.

The transformation, indeed, was more remarkable than he could have believed possible, for respectability itself would seem to have been regained by a costume, and the abundance of her remarkable hair was now repressed. The absence of paint made her cheeks strangely white, the hollows under the eyes darker. The eyes themselves alone betrayed the woman of yesterday; they still burned.

"Why," he exclaimed, looking around him, "you have been busy, haven't you?"

"I've been up since six," she told him proudly. The flat had been dismantled of its meagre furniture, the rug was rolled up and tied, and a trunk strapped with rope was in the middle of the floor. Her next remark brought home to him the full responsibility of his situation. She led him to the window, and pointed to a spot among the drenched weeds and rubbish in the yard next door. "Do you see that bottle? That's the first thing I did - flung it out there. It didn't break," she added significantly, "and there are three drinks in it yet."

Once more he confined his approval to his glance.

"Now you must come and have some breakfast," he said briskly. "If I had thought about it I should have waited to have it with you."

"I'm not hungry." In the light of his new knowledge, he connected her sudden dejection with the sight of the bottle.

"But you must eat. You're exhausted from all this work. And a cup of coffee will make all the difference in the world."

She yielded, pinning on her hat. And he led her, holding the umbrella over her, to a restaurant in Tower Street, where a man in a white cap and apron was baking cakes behind a plate-glass window. She drank the coffee, but in her excitement left the rest of the breakfast almost untasted.

"Say," she asked him once, "why are you doing this?"

"I don't know," he answered, "except that it gives me pleasure."

"Pleasure?"

"Yes. It makes me feel as if I were of some use."

She considered this.

"Well," she observed, reviled by the coffee, "you're the queerest minister I ever saw."

When they had reached the pavement she asked him where they were going.

"To see a friend of mine, and a friend of yours," he told her. "He does net live far from here."

She was silent again, acquiescing. The rain had stopped, the sun was peeping out furtively through the clouds, the early loiterers in Dalton Street stared at them curiously. But Hodder was thinking of that house whither they were bound with a new gratitude, a new wonder that it should exist. Thus they came to the sheltered vestibule with its glistening white paint, its polished name plate and doorknob. The grinning, hospitable darky appeared in answer to the rector's ring.

"Good morning, Sam," he said; "is Mr. Bentley in?"

Sam ushered them ceremoniously into the library, and gate Marcy gazed about her with awe, as at something absolutely foreign to her experience: the New Barrington Hotel, the latest pride of the city, recently erected at the corner of Tower and Jefferson and furnished in the French style, she might partially have understood. Had she been marvellously and suddenly transported and established there, existence might still have evinced a certain continuity. But this house! . .

Mr. Bentley rose from the desk in the corner.

"Oh, it's you, Hodder," he said cheerfully, laying his hand on the rector's arm. "I was just thinking about you."

"This is Miss Marcy, Mr. Bentley," Hodder said.

Mr. Bentley took her hand and led her to a chair.

"Mr. Hodder knows how fond I am of young women," he said. "I have six of them upstairs, - so I am never lonely."

Mr. Bentley did not appear to notice that her lips quivered.

Hodder turned his eyes from her face. "Miss Marcy has

been lonely," he explained, "and I thought we might get her a room near by, where she might see them often. She is going to do embroidery."

"Why, Sally will know of a room," Mr. Bentley replied. "Sam!" he called.

"Yessah - yes, Mistah Ho'ace." Sam appeared at the door.

Ask Miss Sally to come down, if she's not busy."

Kate Marcy sat dumbly in her chair, her hands convulsively clasping its arms, her breast heaving stormily, her face becoming intense with the effort of repressing the wild emotion within her: emotion that threatened to strangle her if resisted, or to sweep her out like a tide and drown her in deep waters: emotion that had no one mewing, and yet summed up a life, mysteriously and overwhelmingly aroused by the sight of a room, and of a kindly old gentleman who lived in it!

Mr. Bentley took the chair beside her.

"Why, I believe it's going to clear off, after all," he exclaimed. "Sam predicted it, before breakfast. He pretends to be able to tell by the flowers. After a while I must show you my flowers, Miss Marcy, and what Dalton Street can do by way of a garden - Mr. Hodder could hardly believe it, even when he saw it." Thus he went on, the tips of his fingers pressed together, his head bent forward in familiar attitude, his face lighted, speaking naturally of trivial things that seemed to suggest themselves; and careful, with exquisite tact that did not betray itself, to address both. A passing automobile startled her with the blast of its horn. "I'm afraid I shall never get accustomed to them," he lamented. "At first I used to be thankful there were no trolley cars on this street, but I believe the automobiles are worse."

A figure flitted through the hall and into the room, which Hodder recognized as Miss Grower's. She reminded him of a flying shuttle across the warp of Mr. Bentley's threads, weaving them together; swift, sure, yet never hurried or flustered. One glance at the speechless woman seemed to suffice her for a knowledge of the situation.

"Mr. Hodder has brought us a new friend and neighbour, Sally, - Miss Kate Marcy. She is to have a room near us, that we may see her often."

Hodder watched Miss Grower's procedure with a breathless interest.

"Why, Mrs. McQuillen has a room - across the street, you know, Mr. Bentley."

Sally perched herself on the edge of the armchair and laid her hand lightly on Kate Marcy's.

Even Sally Grover was powerless to prevent the inevitable, and the touch of her hand seemed the signal for the release of the pent-up forces. The worn body, the worn nerves, the weakened will gave way, and Kate Marcy burst into a paroxysm of weeping that gradually became automatic, convulsive, like a child's. There was no damming this torrent, once released. Kindness, disinterested friendship, was the one unbearable thing.

"We must bring her upstairs," said Sally Grover, quietly, "she's going to pieces."

Hodder helping, they fairly carried her up the flight, and laid her on Sally Grover's own bed.

That afternoon she was taken to Mrs. McQuillen's.

The fiends are not easily cheated. And during the nights and days that followed even Sally Grower, whose slight frame was tireless, whose stoicism was amazing, came out of the sick room with a white face and compressed lips. Tossing on the mattress, Kate Marcy enacted over again incident after incident of her past life, events natural to an existence which had been largely devoid of self-pity, but which now, clearly enough, tested the extreme limits of suffering. Once more, in her visions, she walked the streets, wearily measuring the dark, empty blocks, footsore, into the smaller hours of the night; slyly, insinuatingly, pathetically offering herself - all she possessed - to the hovering beasts of prey. And even these rejected her, with gibes, with obscene jests that sprang to her lips and brought a shudder to those who heard.

Sometimes they beheld flare up fitfully that mysterious thing called the human spirit, which all this crushing process had not served to extinguish. She seemed to be defending her rights, whatever these may have been! She expostulated with policemen. And once, when Hodder was present, she brought back vividly to his mind that first night he had seen her, when she had defied him and sent him away. In moments she lived over again the careless, reckless days when money and good looks had not been lacking, when rich food and wines had been plentiful. And there were other events which Sally Grower and the good-natured Irishwoman, Mrs. McQuillen, not holding the key, could but dimly comprehend. Education, environment, inheritance, character - what a jumble of causes! What Judge was to unravel them, and assign the exact amount of responsibility?

There were other terrible scenes when, more than semiconscious, she cried out piteously for drink, and cursed them for withholding it. And it was in the midst of one of these that an incident occurred which made a deep impression upon young Dr. Giddings, hesitating with his opiates, and assisting the indomitable Miss Grower to hold his patient. In the midst of the paroxysm Mr. Bentley entered and stood over her by the bedside, and suddenly her struggles ceased. At first she lay intensely still, staring at him with wide eyes of fear. He sat down and took her hand, and spoke to her, quietly and naturally, and her pupils relaxed. She fell into a sleep, still clinging to his fingers.

It was Sally who opposed the doctor's wish to send her to a hospital.

"If it's only a question of getting back her health, she'd better die," she declared. "We've got but one chance with her, Dr. Giddings, to keep her here. When she finds out she's been to a hospital, that will be the end of it with her kind. We'll never get hold of her again. I'll take care of Mrs. McQuillen."

Doctor Giddings was impressed by this wisdom.

"You think you have a chance, Miss Grower?" he asked. He had had a hospital experience.

Miss Grower was wont to express optimism in deeds rather than words.

"If I didn't think so, I'd ask you to put a little more in your hypodermic next time," she replied.

And the doctor went away, wondering . . . .

Drink! Convalescence brought little release for the watchers. The fiends would retire, pretending to have abandoned the field, only to swoop down again when least expected. There were periods of calm when it seemed as though a new and bewildered personality were emerging, amazed to find in life a kindly thing, gazing at the world as one new-born. And again, Mrs. McQuillen or Ella Finley might be seen running bareheaded across the street for Miss Grower. Physical force was needed, as the rector discovered on one occasion; physical force, and something more, a dauntlessness that kept Sally Grower in the room after the other women had fled in terror. Then remorse, despondency, another fear . . . .

As the weeks went by, the relapses certainly became fewer. Something was at work, as real in its effects as the sunlight, but invisible. Hodder felt it, and watched in suspense while it fought the beasts in this woman, rending her frame in anguish. The frame might succumb, the breath might leave it to moulder, but the struggle, he knew, would go until the beasts were conquered. Whence this knowledge? - for it was knowledge.

On the quieter days of her convalescence she seemed, indeed, more Madonna than Magdalen as she sat against the pillows, her red-gold hair lying in two heavy plaits across her shoulders, her cheeks pale; the inner, consuming fires that smouldered in her eyes died down. At such times her newly awakened innocence (if it might be called such - pathetic innocence, in truth!) struck awe into Hodder; her wonder was matched by his own. Could there be another meaning in life than the pursuit of pleasure, than the weary effort to keep the body alive?

Such was her query, unformulated. What animated these persons who had struggled over her so desperately, Sally Grower, Mr. Bentley, and Hodder himself? Thus her opening mind. For she had a mind.

Mr. Bentley was the chief topic, and little by little he became exalted into a mystery of which she sought the explanation.

"I never knew anybody like him," she would exclaim.

"Why, I'd seen him on Dalton Street with the children following him, and I saw him again that day of the funeral. Some of the girls I knew used to laugh at him. We thought he was queer. And then, when you brought me to him that morning and he got up and treated me like a lady, I just couldn't stand it. I never felt so terrible in my life. I just wanted to die, right then and there. Something inside of me kept pressing and pressing, until I thought I would die. I knew what it was to hate myself, but I never hated myself as I have since then.

"He never says anything about God, and you don't, but when he comes in here he seems like God to me. He's so peaceful, - he makes me peaceful. I remember the minister in Madison, - he was a putty-faced man with indigestion, - and when he prayed he used to close his eyes and try to look pious, but he never fooled me. He never made me believe he knew anything about God. And don't think for a minute he'd have done what you and Miss Grower and Mr. Bentley did! He used to cross the street to get out of the way of drunken men - he wouldn't have one of them in his church. And I know of a girl he drove out of town because she had a baby and her sweetheart wouldn't marry her. He sent her to hell. Hell's here - isn't it?"

These sudden remarks of hers surprised and troubled him. But they had another effect, a constructive effect. He was astonished, in going over such conversations afterwards, to discover that her questions and his efforts to answer them in other than theological terms were both illuminating and stimulating. Sayings in the Gospels leaped out in his mind, fired with new meanings; so simple, once perceived, that he was amazed not to have seen them before. And then he was conscious of a palpitating joy which left in its wake a profound thankfulness. He made no attempt as yet to correlate these increments, these glimpses of truth into a system, but stored them preciously away.

He taxed his heart and intellect to answer her sensible and helpfully, and thus found himself avoiding the logic, the Greek philosophy, the outworn and meaningless phrases of speculation; found himself employing (with extraordinary effect upon them both) the simple words from which many of these theories had been derived. "He that hath seen me hath seen the Father." What she saw in Horace Bentley, he explained, was God. God wished us to know how to live, in order that we might find happiness, and therefore Christ taught us that the way to find happiness was to teach others how to live, - once we found out. Such was the meaning of Christ's Incarnation, to teach us how to live in order that we might find God and happiness. And Hodder translated for her the word Incarnation.

Now, he asked, how were we to recognize God, how might we know how he wished us to live, unless we saw him in human beings, in the souls into which he had entered? In Mr. Bentley's soul? Was this too deep?

She pondered, with flushed face.

"I never had it put to me like that," she said, presently. "I never could have known what you meant if I hadn't seen Mr. Bentley."

Here was a return flash, for him. Thus, teaching he taught. From this germ he was to evolve for himself the sublime truth that the world grown better, not through automatic, soul-saving machinery, but by Personality.

On another occasion she inquired about "original sin;" - a phrase which had stuck in her memory since the stormings of the Madison preacher. Here was a demand to try his mettle.

"It means," he replied after a moment, "that we are all apt to follow the selfish, animal instincts of our matures, to get all we can for ourselves without thinking of others, to seek animal pleasures. And we always suffer for it."

"Sure," she agreed. "That's what happened to me."

"And unless we see and know some one like Mr.

Bentley," he went on, choosing his words, "or discover for ourselves what Christ was, and what he tried to tell us, we go on 'suffering, because we don't see any way out. We suffer because we feel that we are useless, that other persons are doing our work."

"That's what hell is!" She was very keen. "Hell's here," she repeated.

"Hell may begin here, and so may heaven," he answered.

"Why, he's in heaven now!" she exclaimed, "it's funny I never thought of it before." Of course she referred to Mr. Bentley.

Thus; by no accountable process of reasoning, he stumbled into the path which was to lead him to one of the widest and brightest of his vistas, the secret of eternity hidden in the Parable of the Talents! But it will not do to anticipate this matter . . . .

The divine in this woman of the streets regenerated by the divine in her fellow-creatures, was gasping like a new-born babe for breath. And with what anxiety they watched her! She grew strong again, went with Sally Drover and the other girls on Sunday excursions to the country, applied herself to her embroidery with restless zeal for days, only to have it drop from her nerveless fingers. But her thoughts were uncontrollable, she was drawn continually to the edge of that precipice which hung over the waters whence they had dragged her, never knowing when the vertigo would seize her. And once Sally Drover, on the alert for just such an occurrence, pursued her down Dalton Street and forced her back . . .

Justice to Miss Drover cannot be done in these pages. It was she who bore the brunt of the fierce resentment of the reincarnated fiends when the other women shrank back in fear, and said nothing to Mr. Bentley or Hodder until the incident was past. It was terrible indeed to behold this woman revert - almost in the twinkling of an eye - to a vicious wretch crazed for drink, to feel that the struggle had to be fought all over again. Unable to awe Sally Drover's spirit, she would grow piteous.

"For God's sake let me go - I can't stand it. Let me go to hell - that's where I belong. What do you bother with me for? I've got a right."

Once the doctor had to be called. He shook his head. but his eye met Miss Grower's, and he said nothing.

"I'll never be able to pull out, I haven't got the strength," she told Hodder, between sobs. "You ought to have left me be, that was where I belonged. I can't stand it, I tell you. If it wasn't for that woman watching me downstairs, and Sally Grower, I'd have had a drink before this. It ain't any use, I've got so I can't live without it - I don't want to live."

And then remorse, self-reproach, despair, - almost as terrible to contemplate. She swore she would never see Mr. Bentley again, she couldn't face him.

Yet they persisted, and gained ground. She did see Mr. Bentley, but what he said to her, or she to him, will never be known. She didn't speak of it . . . .

Little by little her interest was aroused, her pride in her work stimulated. None was more surprised than

Hodder when Sally Grower informed him that the embroidery was really good; but it was thought best, for psychological reasons, to discard the old table-cover with its associations and begin a new one. On occasional evenings she brought her sewing over to Mr. Bentley's, while Sally read aloud to him and the young women in the library. Miss Grower's taste in fiction was romantic; her voice (save in the love passages, when she forgot herself) sing-song, but new and unsuspected realms were opened up for Kate Marcy, who would drop her work and gaze wide-eyed out of the window, into the darkness.

And it was Sally who must be given credit for the great experiment, although she took Mr. Bentley and Hodder into her confidence. On it they staked all. The day came, at last, when the new table-cover was finished. Miss Grower took it to the Woman's Exchange, actually sold it, and brought back the money and handed it to her with a smile, and left her alone.

An hour passed. At the end of it Kate Marcy came out of her room, crossed the street, and knocked at the door of Mr. Bentley's library. Hodder happened to be there.

"Come in," Mr. Bentley said.

She entered, breathless, pale. Her eyes, which had already lost much of the dissipated look, were alight with exaltation. Her face bore evidence of the severity of the hour of conflict, and she was perilously near to tears. She handed Mr. Bentley the money.

"What's this, Kate?" he asked, in his kindly way.

"It's what I earned, sir," she faltered. "Miss Grower sold the table-cover. I thought maybe you'd put it aside for me, like you do for the others.

"I'll take good care of it," he said.

"Oh, sir, I don't ever expect to repay you, and Miss Grower and Mr. Hodder!

"Why, you are repaying us," he replied, cutting her short, "you are making us all very happy. And Sally tells me at the Exchange they like your work so well they are asking for more. I shouldn't have suspected," he added, with a humorous glance at the rector, "that Mr. Hodder knew so much about embroidery."

He rose, and put the money in his desk, - such was his genius for avoiding situations which threatened to become emotional.

"I've started another one," she told them, as she departed.

A few moments later Miss Grower appeared.

"Sally," said Mr. Bentley, "you're a wise woman. I believe I've made that remark before. You have managed that case wonderfully."

"There was a time," replied Miss Grower, thoughtfully, when it looked pretty black. We've got a chance with her now, I think."

"I hope so. I begin to feel so," Mr. Bentley declared.

"If we succeed," Miss Grower went on, "it will be

through the heart. And if we lose her again, it will be through the heart."

Hodder started at this proof of insight.

"You know her history, Mr. Hodder?" she asked.

"Yes," he said.

"Well, I don't. And I don't care to. But the way to get at Kate Marcy, light as she is in some respects, is through her feelings. And she's somehow kept 'em alive. We've got to trust her, from now on - that's the only way. And that's what God does, anyhow."

This was one of Miss Grover's rare references to the Deity.

Turning over that phrase in his mind, Hodder went slowly back towards the parish house. God trusted individuals - even such as Kate Marcy. What did that mean? Individual responsibility! He repeated it. Was the world on that principle, then? It was as though a search-light were flung ahead of him and he saw, dimly, a new order - a new order in government and religion. And, as though spoken by a voice out of the past, there sounded in his ears the text of that sermon which had so deeply moved him, "I will arise and go to my Father."

The church was still open, and under the influence of the same strange excitement which had driven him to walk in the rain so long ago, he entered and went slowly up the marble aisle. Through the gathering gloom he saw the figure on the cross. And as he stood gazing at it, a message for which he had been waiting blazed up within him.

He would not leave the Church!

CHAPTER XVIII

THE RIDDLE OF CAUSATION

I

In order to portray this crisis in the life of Kate Marcy, the outcome of which is still uncertain, other matters have been ignored.

How many persons besides John Hodder have seemed to read - in crucial periods - a meaning into incidents having all the outward appearance of accidents! What is it that leads us to a certain man or woman at a certain time, or to open a certain book? Order and design? or influence?

The night when he had stumbled into the cafe in Dalton Street might well have been termed the nadir of Hodder's experience. His faith had been blotted out, and, with it had suddenly been extinguished all spiritual sense, The beast had taken possession. And then, when it was least expected, - nay, when despaired of, had come the glimmer of a light; distant, yet clear. He might have traced the course of his disillusionment, perhaps, but cause and effect were not discernible here.

They soon became so, and in the weeks that followed he grew to have the odd sense of a guiding hand on his shoulder, - such was his instinctive interpretation of it, rather than the materialistic one of things ordained. He might turn, in obedience to what seemed a whim, either to the right or left, only to recognize new blazes that led him on with surer step; and trivial accidents became events charged with meaning. He lived in continual wonder.

One broiling morning, for instance, he gathered up the last of the books whose contents he had a month before so feverishly absorbed, and which had purged him of all fallacies. At first he had welcomed them with a fierce relief, sucked them dry, then looked upon them with loathing. Now he pressed them gratefully, almost tenderly, as he made his way along the shady side of the street towards the great library set in its little park.

He was reminded, as he passed from the blinding sunlight into the cool entrance hall, with its polished marble stairway and its statuary, that Eldon Parr's munificence had made the building possible: that some day Mr. Parr's bust would stand m that vestibule with that of Judge Henry Goodrich - Philip Goodrich's grandfather - and of other men who had served their city and their commonwealth.

Upstairs, at the desk, he was handing in the volumes to the young woman whose duty it was to receive them when he was hailed by a brisk little man in an alpaca coat, with a skin like brown parchment.

"Why, Mr. Hodder," he exclaimed cheerfully, with a trace of German accent, "I had an idea you were somewhere on the cool seas with our friend, Mr. Parr. He spoke, before he left, of inviting you."

It had been Eldon Parr, indeed, who had first brought Hodder to the library, shortly after the rector's advent, and Mr. Engel had accompanied them on a tour of inspection; the financier himself had enjoined the librarian to "take good care" of the clergyman. Mr. Waring, Mr. Atterbury; and Mr. Constable were likewise trustees. And since then, when talking to him, Hodder had had a feeling that Mr. Engel was not unconscious of the aura - if it may be called such - of his vestry.

Mr. Engel picked up one of the books as it lay on the counter, and as he read the title his face betrayed a slight surprise.

"Modern criticism!" he exclaimed.

"You have found me out," the rector acknowledged, smiling.

"Came into my room, and have a chat," said the librarian, coaxingly.

It was a large chamber at the corner of the building, shaded by awnings, against which brushed the branches of an elm which had belonged to the original park. In the centre of the room was a massive oak desk, one whole side of which was piled high with new volumes.

"Look there," said the librarian, with a quick wave of his hand, "those are some which came in this week, and I had them put here to look over. Two-thirds of 'em on religion, or religious philosophy. Does that suggest anything to you clergymen?"

"Do many persons read them, Mr. Engel?" said the rector, at length.

"Read them!" cried Mr. Engel, quizzically. "We librarians are a sort of weather-vanes, if people only knew enough to consult us. We can hardly get a sufficient number of these new religious books the good ones, I mean - to supply the demand. And the Lord knows what trash is devoured, from what the booksellers tell me. It reminds me of the days when this library was down on Fifth Street, years ago, and we couldn't supply enough Darwins and Huxleys and Spencers and popular science generally. That was an agnostic age. But now you'd be surprised to see the different kinds of men and women who come demanding books on religion - all sorts and conditions. They're beginning to miss it out of their lives; they want to know. If my opinion's worth anything, I should not hesitate to declare that we're on the threshold of a greater religious era than the world has ever seen."

Hodder thrust a book back into the pile, and turned abruptly, with a manner that surprised the librarian. No other clergyman to whom he had spoken on this subject had given evidence of this strong feeling, and the rector of St. John's was the last man from whom he would have expected it.

"Do you really think so?" Hodder demanded.

"Why, yes," said Mr. Engel, when he had recovered from his astonishment. "I'm sure of it. I think clergymen especially - if you will pardon me - are apt to forget that this is a reading age. That a great many people who used to get what instruction they had - ahem - from churches, for instance, now get it from books. I don't want to say anything to offend you, Mr. Hodder - "

"You couldn't," interrupted the rector. He was equally surprised at the discovery that he had misjudged Mr. Engel, and was drawn towards him now with a strong sympathy and curiosity.

"Well," replied Mr. Engel, "I'm glad to hear you say that." He restrained a gasp. Was this the orthodox Mr. Hodder of St. John's?

"Why," said Hodder, sitting down, "I've learned, as you have, by experience. Only my experience hasn't been so hopeful as yours - that is, if you regard yours as hopeful. It would be hypocritical of me not to acknowledge that the churches are losing ground, and that those who ought to be connected with them are not. I am ready to admit that the churches are at fault. But what you tell me of people reading these books gives me more courage than I have had for - for some time."

"Is it so!" ejaculated the little man, relapsing into the German idiom of his youth.

"It is," answered the rector, with an emphasis not to be denied. "I wish you would give me your theory about this phenomenon, and speak frankly."

"But I thought - " the bewildered librarian began. "I saw you had been reading those books, but I thought - "

"Naturally you did," said Holder, smiling. His personality, his ascendency, his poise, suddenly felt by the other, were still more confusing. "You thought me a narrow, complacent, fashionable priest who had no concern as to what happened outside the walls of his church, who stuck obstinately to dogmas and would give nothing else a hearing. Well, you were right."

"Ah, I didn't think all that," Mr. Engel protested, and his parchment skin actually performed the miracle of flushing. "I am not so stupid. And once, long ago when I was young, I was going to be a minister myself."

"What prevented you?" asked Holder, interested.

"You want me to be frank - yes, well, I couldn't take the vows." The brown eyes of the quiet, humorous, self-contained and dried-up custodian of the city's reading flamed up. "I felt the call," he exclaimed. "You may not credit it to look at me now, Mr. Hodder. They said to me, 'here is what you must swear to believe before you can make men and women happier and more hopeful, rescue them from sin and misery!' You know what it was."

Hodder nodded.

"It was a crime. It had nothing to do with religion. I thought it over for a year - I couldn't. Oh, I have since been thankful. I can see now what would have happened to me - I should have had fatty degeneration of the soul."

The expression was not merely forcible, it was overwhelming. It brought up before Holder's mind, with sickening reality, the fate he had himself escaped. Fatty degeneration of the soul!

The little man, seeing the expression on the rector's face, curbed his excitement, and feared he had gone too far.

"You will pardon me!" he said penitently, "I forget myself. I did not mean all clergymen."

"I have never heard it put so well," Holder declared. "That is exactly what occurs in many cases."

"Yes, it is that," said Engel, still puzzled, but encouraged, eyeing the strong face of the other. "And they lament that the ministry hasn't more big men. Sometimes they get one with the doctrinal type of mind - a Newman - but how often? And even a Newman would be of little avail to-day. It is Eucken who says that the individual, once released from external authority, can never be turned back to it. And they have been released by the hundreds of thousands ever since Luther's time, are being freed by the hundreds of thousands to-day. Democracy, learning, science, are releasing them, and no man, no matter how great he may be, can stem that tide. The able men in the churches now - like your Phillips Brooks, who died too soon - are beginning to see this. They are those who developed after the vows of the theological schools were behind them. Remove those vows, and you will see the young men come. Young men are idealists, Mr. Hodder, and they embrace other professions where the mind is free, and which are not one whit better paid than the ministry.

"And what is the result," he cried, "of the senseless insistence on the letter instead of the spirit of the poetry of religion? Matthew Arnold was a thousand times right when he inferred that Jesus Christ never spoke literally and yet he is still being taken literally by most churches, and all the literal sayings which were put into his mouth are maintained as Gospel truth! What is the result of proclaiming Christianity in terms of an ancient science and theology which awaken no quickening response in the minds and hearts of to-day? That!" The librarian thrust a yellow hand towards the pile of books. "The new wine has burst the old skin and is running all over the world. Ah, my friend, if you could only see, as I do, the yearning for a satisfying religion which exists in this big city! It is like a vacuum, and those books are rushing to supply it. I little thought," he added dreamily, "when I renounced the ministry in so much sorrow that one day I should have a church of my own. This library is my church, and men and women of all creeds come here by the thousands. But you must pardon me. I have been carried away - I forgot myself."

"Mr. Engel," replied the rector, "I want you to regard me as one of your parishioners."

The librarian looked at him mutely, and the practical, desiccated little person seemed startlingly transformed into a mediaeval, German mystic.

"You are a great man, Mr. Hodder," he said. "I might have guessed it."

It was one of the moments when protest would have been trite, superfluous. And Hodder, in truth, felt something great swelling within him, something that was not himself, and yet strangely was. But just what - in view of his past strict orthodoxy and limited congregation - Mr. Engel meant, he could not have said. Had the librarian recognized, without confession on his part, the change in him? divined his future intentions?

"It is curious that I should have met you this morning, Mr. Engel," he said. "I expressed surprise when you declared this was a religious age, because you corroborated something I had felt, but of which I had no sufficient proof. I felt that a great body of unsatisfied men and women existed, but that I was powerless to get in touch with them; I had discovered that truth, as you have so ably pointed out, is disguised and distorted by ancient dogmas; and that the old Authority, as you say, no longer carries weight."

"Have you found the new one?" Mr. Engel demanded.

"I think I have," the rector answered calmly, "it lies in personality. I do not know whether you will agree with me that the Church at large has a future, and I will confess to you that there was a time when I thought she had not. I see now that she has, once given to her ministers that freedom to develop of which you speak. In spite of the fact that truth has gradually been revealed to the world by what may be called an Apostolic Succession of Personalities, - Augustine, Dante, Francis of Assisi, Luther, Shakespeare, Milton, and our own Lincoln and Phillips Brooks, - to mention only a few, - the Church as a whole has been blind to it. She has insisted upon putting the individual in a straitjacket, she has never recognized that growth is the secret of life, that the clothes of one man are binding on another."

"Ah, you are right - a thousand times right," cried the librarian. "You have read Royce, perhaps, when he says, 'This mortal shall put on individuality - '"

"No," said the rector, outwardly cool, but inwardly excited by the coruscation of this magnificent paraphrase of Paul's sentence, by the extraordinary turn the conversation had taken. "I am ashamed to own that I have not followed the development of modern philosophy. The books I have just returned, on historical criticism," he went on, after a moment's hesitation, "infer what my attitude has been toward modern thought. We were made acquainted with historical criticism in the theological seminary, but we were also taught to discount it. I have discounted it, refrained from reading it, - until now. And yet I have heard it discussed in conferences, glanced over articles in the reviews. I had, you see, closed the door of my mind. I was in a state where arguments make no impression."

The librarian made a gesture of sympathetic assent, which was also a tribute to the clergyman's frankness.

"You will perhaps wonder how I could have lived these years in an atmosphere of modern thought and have remained uninfluenced. Well, I have recently been wondering - myself." Hodder smiled. "The name of Royce is by no means unfamiliar to me, and he taught at Harvard when I was an undergraduate. But the prevailing philosophy of that day among the students was naturalism. I represent a revolt from it. At the seminary I imbibed a certain amount of religious philosophy - but I did not continue it, as thousands of my more liberal fellow-clergymen have done. My religion 'worked' during the time, at least, I remained in my first parish. I had no interest in reconciling, for instance, the doctrine of evolution with the argument for design. Since I have been here in this city," he added, simply, "my days have been filled with a continued perplexity - when I was not too busy to think. Yes, there was an unacknowledged element of fear in my attitude, though I comforted myself with the notion that opinions, philosophical and scientific, were in a state of flux."

"Yes, yes," said Mr. Engel, "I comprehend. But, from the manner in which you spoke just now, I should have inferred that you have been reading modern philosophy - that of the last twenty years. Ah, you have something before you, Mr. Hodder. You will thank God, with me, for that philosophy. It has turned the tide, set the current running the other way. Philosophy is no longer against religion, it is with it. And if you were to ask me to name one of the greatest religious teachers of our age, I should answer, William James. And there is Royce, of whom I spoke, - one of our biggest men. The dominant philosophies of our times have grown up since Arnold wrote his 'Literature and Dogma,' and they are in harmony with the quickening social spirit of the age, which is a religious spirit - a Christian spirit, I call it. Christianity is coming to its own. These philosophies, which are not so far apart, are the flower of the thought of the centuries, of modern science, of that most extraordinary of discoveries, modern psychology. And they are far from excluding religion, from denying the essential of Christ's teachings. On the other hand, they grant that the motive-power of the world is spiritual.

"And this," continued Mr. Engel, "brings me to another aspect of authority. I wonder if it has struck you? In mediaeval times, when a bishop spoke ex cathedra, his authority, so far as it carried weight, came from two sources. First, the supposed divine charter of the Church to save and damn. That authority is being rapidly swept away. Second, he spoke with all the weight of the then accepted science and philosophy. But as soon as the new science began to lay hold on people's minds, as - for instance - when Galileo discovered that the earth moved instead of the sun (and the pope made him take it back), that second authority began to crumble too. In the nineteenth century science had grown so strong that the situation looked hopeless. Religion had apparently irrevocably lost that warrant also, and thinking men not spiritually inclined, since they had to make a choice between science and religion, took science as being the more honest, the more certain.

"And now what has happened? The new philosophies have restored your second Authority, and your first, as you properly say, is replaced by the conception of Personality. Personality is nothing but the rehabilitation of the prophet, the seer. Get him, as Hatch says, back into your Church. The priests with their sacrifices and automatic rites, the logicians, have crowded him out. Why do we read the Old Testament at all? Not for the laws of the Levites, not for the battles and hangings, but for the inspiration of the prophets. The authority of the prophet comes through personality, the source of which is in what Myers calls the infinite spiritual world - in God. It was Christ's own authority.

"And as for your other authority, your ordinary man, when he reads modern philosophy, says to himself, this does not conflict with science? But he gets no hint, when he goes to most churches, that there is, between the two, no real quarrel, and he turns away in despair. He may accept the pragmatism of James, the idealism of Royce, or even what is called neo realism. In any case, he gains the conviction that a force for good is at worn in the world, and he has the incentive to become part of it..... But I have given you a sermon!"

"For which I can never be sufficiently, grateful," said Hodder, with an earnestness not to be mistaken.

The little man's eyes rested admiringly, and not without emotion, on the salient features of the tall clergyman. And when he spoke again, it was in acknowledgment of the fact that he had read Hodder's purpose.

"You will have opposition, my friend. They will fight you - some persons we know. They do not wish - what you and I desire. But you will not surrender - I knew it." Mr. Engel broke off abruptly, and rang a bell on his desk. "I will make out for you a list. I hope you may come in again, often. We shall have other talks, - yes? I am always here."

Then it came to pass that Hodder carried back with him another armful of books. Those he had brought back were the Levellers of the False. These were the Builders of the True.

II

Hodder had known for many years that the writings of Josiah Royce and of William James had "been in the air," so to speak, and he had heard them mentioned at dinner parties by his more intellectual parishioners, such as Mrs. Constable and Martha Preston. Now he was able to smile at his former attitude toward these moderns, whose perusal he had deprecated as treason to the saints! And he remembered his horror on having listened to a fellow-clergyman discuss with calmness the plan of the "Varieties of Religious Experiences." A sacrilegious dissection of the lives of these very saints! The scientific process, the theories of modern psychology applied with sang-froid to the workings of God in the human soul! Science he had regarded as the proclaimed enemy of religion, and in these days of the apotheosis of science not even sacred things were spared.

Now Hodder saw what the little librarian had meant by an authority restored. The impartial method of modern science had become so firmly established in the mind of mankind by education and reading that the ancient unscientific science of the Roman Empire, in which orthodox Christianity was clothed, no longer carried authority. In so far as modern science had discovered truth, religion had no quarrel with it. And if theology pretended to be the science of religion, surely it must submit to the test of the new science! The dogged clinging to the archaic speculations of apologists, saints, and schoolmen had brought religion to a low ebb indeed.

One of the most inspiring books he read was by an English clergyman of his own Church whom he had formerly looked upon as a heretic, with all that the word had once implied. It was a frank yet reverent study of the self-consciousness of Christ, submitting the life and teachings of Jesus to modern criticism and the scientific method. And the Saviour's divinity, rather than being lessened, was augmented. Hodder found it infinitely refreshing that the so-called articles of Christian belief, instead of being put first and their acceptance insisted upon, were made the climax of the investigation.

Religion, he began to perceive, was an undertaking, are attempt to find unity and harmony of the soul by adopting, after mature thought, a definite principle in life. If harmony resulted, - if the principle worked, it was true. Hodder kept an open mind, but he became a pragmatist so far. Science, on the other hand, was in a sphere by herself, and need have no conflict with religion; science was not an undertaking, but an impartial investigation by close observation of facts in nature. Her object was to discover truths by these methods alone. She had her theories, indeed, but they must be submitted to rigorous tests. This from a book by Professor Perry, an advocate of the new realism.

On the other hand there were signs that modern science, by infinitesimal degrees, might be aiding in the solution of the Mystery . . . .

But religion, Hodder saw, was trusting. Not credulous, silly trusting, but thoughtful trusting, accepting such facts as were definitely known. Faith was trusting. And faith without works was dead simply because there could be no faith without works. There was no such thing as belief that did not result in act.

A paragraph which made a profound impression on Hodder at that time occurs in James's essay, "Is life worth living?"

"Now-what do I mean by I trusting? Is the word to carry with it license to define in detail an invisible world, and to authorize and excommunicate those whose trust is different? . . Our faculties of belief were not given us to make orthodoxies and heresies withal; they were given us to live by. And to trust our religions demands men first of all to live in the light of them, and to act as if the invisible world which they suggest were real. It is a fact of human nature that man can live and die by the help of a sort of faith that goes without a single dogma and definition."

Yet it was not these religious philosophies which had saved him, though the stimulus of their current had started his mind revolving like a motor. Their function, he perceived now, was precisely to compel him to see what had saved him, to reenforce it with the intellect, with the reason, and enable him to save others. The current set up, - by a thousand suggestions of which he made notes, - a personal construction, coordination, and he had the exhilaration of feeling, within him, a creative process all his own. Behold a mystery 'a paradox' - one of many. As his strength grew greater day by day, as his vision grew clearer, he must exclaim with Paul: "Yet not I, but the grace of God which was with me!"

He, Hodder, was but an instrument transmitting power. And yet - oh paradox! - the instrument continued to improve, to grow stronger, to develop individuality and personality day by day! Life, present and hereafter, was growth, development, the opportunity for service in a cause. To cease growing was to die.

He perceived at last the form all religion takes is that of consecration to a Cause, - one of God's many causes. The meaning of life is to find one's Cause, to lose one's self in it. His was the liberation of the Word, - now vouchsafed to him; the freeing of the spark from under the ashes. The phrase was Alison's. To help liberate the Church, fan into flame the fire which was to consume the injustice, the tyranny, the selfishness of the world, until the Garvins, the Kate Marcys, the stunted children, and anaemic women were no longer possible.

It was Royce who, in one illuminating sentence, solved for him the puzzle, pointed out whence his salvation had come. "For your cause can only be revealed to you through some presence that first teaches you to love the unity of the spiritual life. . . You must find it in human shape."

Horace Bentley!

He, Hodder, had known this, but known it vaguely, without sanction. The light had shone for him even in the darkness of that night in Dalton Street, when he thought to have lost it forever. And he had awakened the next morning, safe, - safe yet bewildered, like a half drowned man on warm sands in the sun.

"The will of the spiritual world, the divine will, revealed in man." What sublime thoughts, as old as the Cross itself, yet continually and eternally new!

III

There was still another whose face was constantly before him, and the reflection of her distressed yet undaunted soul, - Alison Parr. The contemplation of her courage, of her determination to abide by nothing save the truth, had had a power over him that he might not estimate, and he loved her as a man loves a woman, for her imperfections. And he loved her body and her mind.

One morning, as he walked back from Mrs. Bledsoe's through an unfrequented, wooded path of the Park, he beheld her as he had summoned her in his visions. She was sitting motionless, gazing before her with clear eyes, as at the Fates. . .

She started on suddenly perceiving him, but it was characteristic of her greeting that she seemed to feel no surprise at the accident which had brought them together.

"I am afraid," he said, smiling, "that I have broken in on some profound reflections."

She did not answer at once, but looked up at him, as he stood over her, with one of her strange, baffling gazes, in which there was the hint of a welcoming smile.

"Reflection seems to be a circular process with me," she answered. "I never get anywhere - like you."

"Like me!" he exclaimed, seating himself on the bench. Apparently their intercourse, so long as it should continue, was destined to be on the basis of intimacy in which it had begun. It was possible at once to be aware of her disturbing presence, and yet to feel at home in it.

"Like you, yes," she said, continuing to examine him. "You've changed remarkably."

In his agitation, at this discovery of hers he again repeated her words.

"Why, you seem happier, you look happier. It isn't only that, I can't explain how you impress me. It struck me when you were talking to Mr. Bentley the other day. You seem to see something you didn't see when I first met you, that you didn't see the first time we were at Mr. Bentley's together. Your attitude is fixed - directed. You have made a decision of some sort - a momentous one, I rather think."

"Yes," he replied, "you are right. It's more than remarkable that you should have guessed it."

She remained silent

"I have decided," he found himself saying abruptly, "to continue in the Church."

Still she was silent, until he wondered whether she would answer him. He had often speculated to himself how she would take this decision, but he could make no surmise from her expression as she stared off into the wood. Presently she turned her head, slowly, and looked into his face. Still she did not speak.

"You are wondering how I can do it," he said.

"Yes," she acknowledged, in a low voice.

"I should like you to know - that is why I spoke of it. You have never asked me, and I have never told you that the convictions I formerly held I lost. And with them, for a while, went everything. At least so I believed."

"I knew it," she answered, "I could see that, too."

"When I argued with you, that afternoon, - the last time we talked together alone, - I was trying to convince myself, and you - " he hesitated, " - that there was something. The fact that you could not seem to feel it stimulated me."

He read in her eyes that she understood him. And he dared not, nor did he need to emphasize further his own intense desire that she should find a solution of her own.

"I wish you to know what I am telling you for two reasons," he went on. "It was you who spoke the words that led to the opening of my eyes to the situation into which I had been drifting for two years, who compelled me to look upon the inconsistencies and falsities which had gradually been borne in upon me. It was you, I think, who gave me the courage to face this situation squarely, since you possess that kind of courage yourself."

"Oh, no," she cried. "You would have done it anyway."

He paused a moment, to get himself in hand.

"For this reason, I owed it to you to speak - to thank

you. I have realized, since that first meeting, that you became my friend then, and that you spoke as a friend. If you had not believed in my sincerity, you would not have spoken. I wish you to know that I am fully aware and grateful for the honour you did me, and that I realize it is not always easy for you to speak so - to any one."

She did not reply.

"There is another reason for my telling you now of this decision of mine to remain a clergyman," he continued. "It is because I value your respect and friendship, and I hope you will believe that I would not take this course unless I saw my way clear to do it with sincerity."

"One has only to look at you to see that you are sincere," she said gently, with a thrill in her voice that almost unmanned him. "I told you once that I should never have forgiven myself if I had wrecked your life. I meant it. I am very glad."

It was his turn to be silent.

"Just because I cannot see how it would be possible to remain in the Church after one had been - emancipated, so to speak," - she smiled at him, - "is no reason why you may not have solved the problem."

Such was the superfine quality of her honesty. Yet she trusted him! He was made giddy by a desire, which he fought down, to justify himself before her. His eye beheld her now as the goddess with the scales in her hand, weighing and accepting with outward calm the verdict of the balance . . . . Outward calm, but inner fire.

"It makes no difference," she pursued evenly, bent on choosing her words, "that I cannot personally understand your emancipation, that mine is different. I can only see the preponderance of evil, of deception, of injustice - it is that which shuts out everything else. And it's temperamental, I suppose. By looking at you, as I told you, I can see that your emancipation is positive, while mine remains negative. You have somehow regained a conviction that the good is predominant, that there is some purpose in the universe."

He assented. Once more she relapsed into thought, while he sat contemplating her profile. She turned to him again with a tremulous smile.

"But isn't a conviction that the good is predominant, that there is a purpose in the universe, a long way from the positive assertions in the Creeds?" she asked. "I remember, when I went through what you would probably call disintegration, and which seemed to me enlightenment, that the Creeds were my first stumbling-blocks. It seemed wrong to repeat them."

"I am glad you spoke of this," he replied gravely. "I have arrived at many answers to that difficulty - which did not give me the trouble I had anticipated. In the first place, I am convinced that it was much more of a difficulty ten, twenty, thirty years ago than it is to-day. That which I formerly thought was a radical tendency towards atrophy, the drift of the liberal party in my own Church and others, as well as that which I looked upon with some abhorrence as the free-thinking speculation of many modern writers, I have now come to see is reconstruction. The results of this teaching of religion in modern terms are already becoming apparent, and some persons are already beginning to see that the Creeds express certain elemental truths in frankly archaic language. All this should be explained in the churches and the Sunday schools, - is, in fact, being explained in some, and also in books for popular reading by clergymen of my own Church, both here and in England. We have got past the critical age."

She followed him closely, but did not interrupt.

"I do not mean to say that the Creeds are not the sources of much misunderstanding, but in my opinion they do not constitute a sufficient excuse for any clergyman to abandon his Church on account of them. Indeed there are many who interpret them by modern thought - which is closer to the teachings of Christ than ancient thought - whose honesty cannot be questioned. Personally, I think that the Creeds either ought to be taken out of the service; or changed, or else there should be a note inserted in the service and catechism definitely permitting a liberal interpretation which is exactly what so many clergymen, candidly, do now.

"When I was ordained a deacon, and then a priest, I took vows which would appear to be literally conflicting. Compelled to choose between these vows, I accept that as supreme which I made when I affirmed that I would teach nothing which I should be persuaded might not be concluded and affirmed by the Scripture. The Creeds were derived from the Scripture - not the Scripture from the Creeds. As an individual among a body of Christians I am powerless to change either the ordinal vows or the Creeds, I am obliged to wait for the consensus of opinion. But if, on the whole, I can satisfy my conscience in repeating the Creeds and reading the service, as other honest men are doing - if I am convinced that I have an obvious work to do in that Church, it would be cowardly for me to abandon that work."

Her eyes lighted up.

"I see what you mean," she said, "by staying in you can do many things that you could not do, you can help to bring about the change, by being frank. That is your point of view. You believe m the future of the Church."

"I believe in an universal, Christian organization," he replied.

"But while stronger men are honest," she objected, "are not your ancient vows and ancient Creeds continually making weaker men casuists?"

"Undoubtedly," he agreed vigorously, and thought involuntarily of Mr. Engel's phrased fatty degeneration of the soul. "Yet I can see the signs, on all sides, of a gradual emancipation, of which I might be deemed an example." A smile came into his eyes, like the sun on a grey-green sea.

"Oh, you could never be a casuist!" she exclaimed, with a touch of vehemence. "You are much too positive. It is just that note, which is characteristic of so many clergymen, that note of smoothing-over and apology, which you lack. I could never feel it, even when you were orthodox. And now - " words failed her as she inspected his ruggedness.

"And now," he took her up, to cover his emotion, "now I am not to be classified!"

Still examining him, she reflected on this.

"Classified?" Isn't it because you're so much of an individual that one fails to classify you? You represent something new to my experience, something which seems almost a contradiction - an emancipated Church."

"You imagined me out of the Church, - but where?" he demanded.

"That's just it," she wondered intimately, "where? When I try, I can see no other place for you. Your place as in the pulpit."

He uttered a sharp exclamation, which she did not heed.

"I can't imagine you doing institutional work, as it is called, - you're not fitted for it, you'd be wasted in it. You gain by the historic setting of the Church, and yet it does not absorb you. Free to preach your convictions, unfettered, you will have a power over people that will be tremendous. You have a very strong personality."

She set his heart, his mind, to leaping by this unexpected confirmation on her part of his hopes, and yet the man in him was intent upon the woman. She had now the air of detached judgment, while he could not refrain from speculating anxiously on the effect of his future course on her and on their intimate relationship. He forbore from thinking, now, of the looming events which might thrust them apart, - put a physical distance between them, - his anxiety was concerned with the possible snapping of the thread of sympathy which had bound them. In this respect, he dreaded her own future as much as his own. What might she do? For he felt, in her, a potential element of desperation; a capacity to commit, at any moment, an irretrievable act.

"Once you have made your ideas your own," she mused, "you will have the power of convincing people."

"And yet - "

"And yet" - she seized his unfinished sentence, "you are not at all positive of convincing me. I'll give you the credit of forbearing to make proselytes." She smiled at him.

Thus she read him again.

"If you call making proselytes a desire to communicate a view of life which gives satisfaction - " he began, in his serious way.

"Oh, I want to be convinced!" she exclaimed, penitently, "I'd give anything to feel as you feel. There's something lacking in me, there must be, and I have only seen the disillusionizing side. You infer that the issue of the Creeds will crumble, - preach the new, and the old will fall away of itself. But what is the new? How, practically, do you deal with the Creeds? We have got off that subject."

"You wish to know?" he asked.

"Yes - I wish to know."

"The test of any doctrine is whether it can be translated into life, whether it will make any difference to the individual who accepts it. The doctrines expressed in the Creeds must stand or fall by the test. Consider, for instance, the fundamental doctrine in the Creeds, that of the Trinity, which has been much scoffed at. A belief in God, you will admit, has an influence on conduct, and the Trinity defines the three chief aspects of the God in whom Christians believe. Of what use to quarrel with the word Person if God be conscious? And the character of God has an influence on conduct. The ancients deemed him wrathful, jealous, arbitrary, and hence flung themselves before him and propitiated him. If the conscious God of the universe be good, he is spoken of as a Father. He is as once, in this belief, Father and Creator. And inasmuch as it is known that the divine qualities enter into man, and that one Man, Jesus, whose composite portrait - it is agreed - could not have been factitiously invented, was filled with them, we speak of God in man as the Son. And the Spirit of God that enters into the soul of man, transforming, inspiring, and driving him, is the Third Person, so-called. There is no difficulty so far, granted the initial belief in a beneficent God.

"If we agree that life has a meaning, and, in order to conform to the purpose of the Spirit of the Universe, must be lived in one way, we certainly cannot object to calling that right way of living, that decree of the Spirit, the Word.

"The Incarnate Word, therefore, is the concrete example of a human being completely filled with the Spirit, who lives a perfect life according to its decree. Ancient Greek philosophy called this decree, this meaning of life, the Logos, and the Nicene Creed is a confession of faith in that philosophy. Although this creed is said to have been, scandalously forced through the council of Nicaea by an emperor who had murdered his wife and children, and who himself was unbaptized, against a majority of bishops who would, if they had dared Constantine's displeasure, have given the conscience freer play, to-day the difficulty has, practically disappeared. The creed is there in the prayer book, and so long as it remains we are at liberty to interpret the ancient philosophy in which it is written - and which in any event could not have been greatly improved upon at that time - in our own modern way, as I am trying to explain it to you.

"Christ was identified with the Logos, or Word, which must have had a meaning for all time, before and after its, complete revelation. And this is what the Nicene Creed is trying to express when it says, 'Begotten of his Father before all worlds.' In other words, the purpose which Christ revealed always existed. The awkward expression of the ancients, declaring that he 'came down' for our salvation (enlightenment) contains a fact we may prove by experience, if we accept the meaning he put upon existence, and adopt this meaning as our scheme of life. But we: must first be quite clear, as: to this meaning. We may and do express all this differently, but it has a direct bearing on life. It is the doctrine of the Incarnation. We begins to perceive through it that our own incarnations mean something, and that our task is to discover what they do mean - what part in the world purpose we are designed to play here.

"Incarnate by the Holy Ghost of the Virgin Mary is an emphasis on the fact that man born of woman may be divine. But the ignorant masses of the people of the

Roman Empire were undoubtedly incapable of grasping a theory of the Incarnation put forward in the terms of Greek philosophy; while it was easy for them, with their readiness to believe in nature miracles, to accept the explanation of Christ's unique divinity as due to actual, physical generation by the Spirit. And the wide belief in the Empire in gods born in this way aided such a conception. Many thousands were converted to Christianity when a place was found in that religion for a feminine goddess, and these abandoned the worship of Isis, Demeter, and Diana for that of the Virgin Mary. Thus began an evolution which is still going on, and we see now that it was impossible that the world should understand at once the spiritual meaning of life as Christ taught it - that material facts merely symbolize the divine. For instance, the Gospel of John has been called the philosophical or spiritual gospel. And in spite of the fact that it has been assailed and historically discredited by modern critics, for me it serves to illuminate certain truths of Christ's message and teaching that the other Gospels do not. Mark, the earliest Gospel, does not refer to the miraculous birth. At the commencements of Matthew and Luke you will read of it, and it is to be noted that the rest of these narratives curiously and naively contradict it. Now why do we find the miraculous birth in these Gospels if it had not been inserted in order to prove, in a manner acceptable to simple and unlettered minds, the Theory of the Incarnation, Christ's preexistence? I do not say the insertion was deliberate. And it is difficult for us moderns to realize the polemic spirit in which the Gospels were written. They were clearly not written as history. The concern of the authors, I think, was to convert their readers to Christ.

"When we turn to John, what do we find? In the opening verses of this Gospel the Incarnation is explained, not by a virgin birth, but in a manner acceptable to the educated and spiritually-minded, in terms of the philosophy of the day. And yet how simply! 'In the beginning was the Word, and the Word was with God, and the Word was God.' I prefer John's explanation.

"It is historically true that, in the earlier days when the Apostles' Creed was put forth, the phrase 'born of they Virgin Mary' was inserted for the distinct purpose of laying stress on the humanity of Christ, and to controvert the assertion of the Gnostic sect that he was not born at all, but appeared in the world in some miraculous way.

"Thus to-day, by the aid of historical research, we are enabled to regard the Creeds in the light of their usefulness to life. The myth of the virgin birth probably arose through the zeal of some of the writers of the Gospels to prove that the prophecy of Isaiah predicted the advent of the Jewish Messiah who should be born of a virgin. Modern scholars are agreed that the word Olmah which Isaiah uses does not mean virgin, but young woman. There is quite a different Hebrew word for 'virgin.' The Jews, at the time the Gospels were written, and before, had forgotten their ancient Hebrew. Knowing this mistake, and how it arose, we may repeat the word Virgin Mary in the sense used by many early Christians, as designating the young woman who was the mother of Christ.

"I might mention one or two other phrases, archaic and obscure. 'The Resurrection of the Body' may refer to the phenomenon of Christ's reappearance after death, for which modern psychology may or may not account. A little reflection, however, convinces one that the phenomenon did take place in some manner, or else, I think, we should never have heard of Christ. You will remember that the Apostles fled after his death on the cross, believing what he had told them was all only a dream. They were human, literal and cowardly, and they still needed some kind of inner, energizing conviction that the individuality persisted after death, that the solution of human life was victory over it, in order to gain the courage to go out and preach the Gospel and face death themselves. And it was Paul who was chiefly instrumental in freeing the message from the narrow bounds of Palestine and sending it ringing down the ages to us. The miracle doesn't lie in what Paul saw, but in the whole man transformed, made incandescent, journeying tirelessly to the end of his days up and down the length and breadth of the empire, labouring, as he says, more abundantly than they all. It is idle to say that the thing which can transform a man's entire nature and life is not a reality."

She had listened, motionless, as under the spell of his words. Self-justification, as he proceeded, might easily have fused itself into a desire to convince her of the truth of his beliefs. But he was not deceived, he knew her well enough to understand, to feel the indomitable spirit of resistance in her. Swayed she could be, but she would mot easily surrender.

"There is another phrase," she said after a moment, "which I have never heard explained, 'descended into hell.'"

"It was merely a matter of controverting those who

declared Christ was taken from the cross before he died. In the childish science of the time, to say that one descended into hell was to affirm that he was actually dead, since the souls of the departed were supposed to go at once to hell. Hell and heaven were definite places. To say that Christ ascended to heaven and sat on the right hand of the Father is to declare one's faith that his responsible work in the spiritual realm continues."

"And the Atonement? doesn't that imply a sacrifice of propitiation?"

"Atonement may be pronounced At-one-ment," Hodder replied. "The old idea, illustrated by a reference to the sacrifice of the ancients, fails to convey the truth to modern minds. And moreover, as I have inferred, these matters had to be conveyed in symbols until mankind were prepared to grasp the underlying spiritual truths which Christ sought to convey. Orthodox Christianity has been so profoundly affected by the ancient Jewish religion that the conception of God as wrathful and jealous - a God wholly outside - has persisted to our times. The Atonement means union with the Spirit of the Universe through vicarious suffering, and experience teaches us that our own sufferings are of no account unless they be for a cause, for the furtherance of the design of the beneficent Spirit which is continually at work. Christ may be said to have died for humanity because he had to suffer death itself in order to reveal the complete meaning of life. You once spoke to me about the sense of sin - of being unable to feel it."

She glanced at him quickly, but did not speak.

"There is a theory concerning this," he continued, "which has undoubtedly helped many people, and which may be found in the writings of certain modern psychologists. It is that we have a conscious, or lower, human self, and a subconscious, or better self. This subconscious self stretches down, as it were, into the depths of the universe and taps the source of spiritual power. And it is through the subconscious self that every man is potentially divine. Potentially, because the conscious self has to reach out by an effort of the will to effect this union with the spiritual in the subconscious, and when it is effected, it comes from the response of the subconscious. Apparently from without, as a gift, and therefore, in theological language, it is called grace. This is what is meant by being born again, the incarnation of the Spirit in the conscious, or human. The two selves are no longer divided, and the higher self assumes control, - takes the reins, so to speak.

"It is interesting, as a theory. And the fact that it has been seriously combated by writers who deny such a function of the subconscious does not at all affect the reality of the experience.

"Once we have had a vision of the true meaning of life a vision which stirs the energies of our being, what is called 'a sense of sin' inevitably follows. It is the discontent, the regret, in the light of a higher knowledge, for the: lost opportunities, for a past life which has been uncontrolled by any unifying purpose, misspent in futile undertakings, wasted, perhaps, in follies and selfish caprices which have not only harmed ourselves but others. Although we struggle, yet by habit, by self-indulgence, by lack of a sustained purpose, we have formed a character from which escape seems hopeless. And we realize that in order to change ourselves, an actual regeneration of the will is necessary. For awhile, perchance, we despair of this. The effort to get out of the rut we have made for ourselves seems of no avail. And it is not, indeed, until we arrive, gradually or otherwise, and through a proper interpretation of the life of Christ, at the conviction that we may even never become useful in the divine scheme that we have a sense of what is called 'the forgiveness of sins.' This conviction, this grace, this faith to embark on the experiment accomplishes of itself the revival of the will, the rebirth which we had thought impossible. We discover our task, high or humble, - our cause. We grow marvellously at one with God's purpose, and we feel that our will is acting in the same direction as his. And through our own atonement we see the meaning of that other Atonement which led Christ to the Cross. We see that our conviction, our grace, has come through him, and how he died for our sins."

"It's quite wonderful how logical and simple you make it, how thoroughly yon have gone into it. You have solved it for yourself - and you will solve it for others many others."

She rose, and he, too, got to his feet with a medley of feelings. The path along which they walked was already littered with green acorns. A gray squirrel darted ahead of them, gained a walnut and paused, quivering, halfway up the trunk, to gaze back at them. And the glance she presently gave him seemed to partake of the shyness of the wild thing.

"Thank you for explaining it to me," she said.

"I hope you don't think - " he began.

"Oh, it isn't that!" she cried, with unmistakable reproach. "I asked you - I made you tell me. It hasn't seemed at all like - the confessional," she added, and smiled and blushed at the word. "You have put it so nicely, so naturally, and you have given me so much to think about. But it all depends - doesn't it? - upon whether one can feel the underlying truth of which you spoke in the first place; it rests upon a sense of the prevailing goodness of things. It seems to me cruel that what is called salvation, the solution of the problem of life, should depend upon an accidental discovery. We are all turned loose with our animal passions and instincts, of self-preservation, by an indifferent Creator, in a wilderness, and left to find our way out as best we can. You answer that Christ showed us the way. There are elements in his teaching I cannot accept - perhaps because I have been given a wrong interpretation of them. I shall ask you more questions some day.

"But even then," she continued, "granted that Christ brought the complete solution, as you say, why should so many millions have lived and died, before and after his coming, who had suffered so, and who had never heard of him? That is the way my reason works, and I can't help it. I would help it if I could."

"Isn't it enough," he asked, "to know that a force is at work combating evil, - even if you are not yet convinced that it is a prevailing force? Can you not trust that it will be a prevailing force, if your sympathies are with it, without demanding a revelation of the entire scheme of the universe? Of what use is it to doubt the eternal justice?"

"Oh, use!" she cried, "I grant you its uselessness. Doubt seems an ingrained quality. I can't help being a fatalist."

"And yet you have taken your life in your own hands," he reminded her, gently.

"Only to be convinced of its futility," she replied.

Again, momentarily thrust back into himself, he wondered jealously once more what the disillusionments had been of that experience from before which she seemed, at times, ready to draw back a little the veil.

"A sense of futility is a sense of incompleteness," he said, "and generally precedes a sense of power."

"Ah, you have gained that! Yet it must always have been latent in you - you make one feel it. But now!" she exclaimed, as though the discovery had just dawned on her, "now you will need power, now you will have to fight as you have never fought in your life."

He found her enthusiasm as difficult to withstand as her stoicism.

"Yes, I shall have to fight," he admitted. Her partisanship was sweet.

"When you tell them what you have told me," she continued, as though working it out in her own mind, "they will never submit to it, if they can help it. My father will never submit to it. They will try to put you out, as a heretic, - won't they?"

"I have an idea that they will," he conceded, with a smile.

"And won't they succeed? Haven't they the power?"

"It depends, - in the first place, on whether the bishop thinks me a heretic."

"Have you asked him?"

"No."

"But can't they make you resign?"

"They can deprive me of my salary."

She did not press this.

"You mustn't think me a martyr," he pleaded, in a lighter tone.

She paid no heed to this protest, but continued to regard him with a face lighted by enthusiasm.

"Oh, that's splendid of you!" she cried. "You are going to speak the truth as you see it, and let them do their worst. Of course, fundamentally, it isn't merely because they're orthodox that they won't like it, although they'll say so, and perhaps think so. It will be because if you have really found the truth - they will instinctively, fear its release. For it has a social bearing, too - hasn't it? - although you haven't explained that part of it."

"It has a distinct social bearing," he replied, amazed at the way her mind flew forward and grasped the entire issue, in spite of the fact that her honesty still refused to concede his premises. Such were the contradictions in her that he loved. And, though she did not suspect it, she had in her the Crusader's spirit. "I have always remembered what you once said, that many who believed themselves Christians had an instinctive feeling that there is a spark in Christianity which, if allowed to fly, would start a conflagration beyond their control. And that they had covered the spark with ashes. I, too," he added whimsically, "was buried under the ashes."

"And the spark," she demanded, "is not Socialism - their nightmare?"

"The spark is Christianity itself - but I am afraid they will not be able to distinguish it from Socialism. The central paradox in Christianity consists in the harmonizing of the individual and socialistic spirit, and this removes it as far from the present political doctrine of socialism as it is possible to be. Christianity, looked at from a certain viewpoint, - and I think the proper viewpoint, - is the most individualistic of religions, since its basic principle is the development of the individual into an autonomous being."

They stood facing each other on an open stretch of lawn. The place was deserted. Through the trees, in the near distance, the sightless front of the Ferguson mansion blazed under the September sun.

"Individualistic!" she repeated, as though dazed by the word applied to the religion she had discarded. "I can't understand. Do you think I ever can understand?" she asked him, simply.

"It seems to me you understand more than you are willing to give yourself credit for," he answered seriously. "You don't take into account your attitude."

"I see what you mean - a willingness to take the right road, if I can find it. I am not at all sure that I want to take it. But you must tell me more - more of what you have discovered. Will you?"

He just hesitated. She herself appeared to acknowledge no bar to their further intimacy - why should he?

"I will tell you all I know," he said.

Suddenly, as if by a transference of thought, she voiced what he had in mind.

"You are going to tell them the truth about themselves!" she exclaimed. " - That they are not Christians!"

His silence was an admission.

"You must see," he told her, after the moment they had looked into each other's faces, "that this is the main reason why I must stay at St. John's, in the Church, if I conscientiously can."

"I see. The easier course would be to resign, to have scruples. And you believe there is a future for the Church."

"I believe it," he assented.

She still held his eyes.

"Yes, it is worth doing. If you see it that way it is more worth doing than anything else. Please don't think," she said, "that I don't appreciate why you have told me all this, why you have given me your reasons. I know it hasn't been easy. It's because you wish me to have faith in you for my own sake, not for yours. And I am grateful."

"And if that faith is justified, as you will help to justify it, that it may be transferred to a larger sphere," he answered.

She gave him her hand, but did not reply.

CHAPTER XIX

MR. GOODRICH BECOMES A PARTISAN

I

In these days of his preparation, she haunted him continually. In her he saw typified all those who possessed the: divine discontent, the yearning unsatisfied, - the fatalists and the dreamers. And yet she seemed to have risen through instinct to share the fire of his vision of religion revealed to the countless ranks of strugglers as the hidden motive-power of the world, the impetus of scientist, statesman, artist, and philanthropist! They had stood together on the heights of the larger view, whence the whole of the battle-line lay disclosed.

At other and more poignant moments he saw her as waving him bravely on while he steamed out through towering seas to safety. The impression was that of smiling at her destiny. Had she fixed upon it? and did she linger now only that she might inspire him in his charge? She was capable, he knew, of taking calmly the irrevocable step, of accepting the decree as she read it. The thought tortured, the desire to save her from herself obsessed him; with true clairvoyance she had divined him aright when she had said that he wished her to have faith in him for her own sake. Could he save her in spite of herself? and how? He could not see her, except by chance. Was she waiting until he should have crossed the bar before she should pay some inexorable penalty of which he knew nothing?

Thus he speculated, suffered, was at once cast down and lifted up by the thought of her. To him, at least, she was one of those rare and dauntless women, the red stars of history, by whom the Dantes and Leonardos are fired to express the inexpressible, and common clay is fused and made mad: one of those women who, the more they reveal, become the more inscrutable. Divinely inarticulate, he called her; arousing the passion of the man, yet stirring the sublimer efforts of the god.

What her feelings toward him, whether she loved him as a woman loves a man he could not say, no man being a judge in the supreme instance. She beheld him emancipated, perhaps, from what she might have called the fetters of an orthodoxy for which she felt an instinctive antagonism; but whether, though proclaiming himself free, the fact of his continuation in the ministry would not of itself set up in her a reaction, he was unable to predict. Her antipathy to forms, he saw, was inherent. Her interest - her fascinated absorption, it might be called - in his struggle was spiritual, indeed, but it also had mixed in it the individualistic zeal of the nonconformist. She resented the trammels of society; though she suffered from her efforts to transcend them. The course he had determined upon appeared to her as a rebellion not only against a cut-and-dried state of mind, but also against vested privilege. Yet she had in her, as she confessed, the craving for what privilege brings in the way of harmonious surroundings. He loved her for her contradictions.

Thus he was utterly unable to see what the future held for him in the way of continued communion with her, to evolve any satisfactory theory as to why she remained in the city. She had told him that the gardens were an excuse. She had come, by her own intimation, to reflect, to decide some momentous question. Marriage? He found this too agitating to dwell upon, summoning, as it did, conjectures of the men she might have known; and it was perhaps natural, in view of her attitude, that he could only think of such a decision on her part as surrender.

That he had caught and held her attention, although by no conscious effort of his own, was clear to him. But had he not merely arrested her? Would she not presently disappear, leaving only in his life the scarlet thread which she had woven into it for all time? Would he not fail to change, permanently, the texture of hers?

Such were his hopes and fears concerning her, and they were mingled inextricably with other hopes and fears which had to do with the great venture of his life. He dwelt in a realm of paradoxes, discovered that exaltation was not incompatible with anxiety and dread. He had no thought of wavering; he had achieved to an extent he would not have believed possible the sense of consecration which brings with it indifference to personal fortunes, and the revelation of the inner world, and yet he shrank from the wounds he was about to receive - and give. Out wardly controlled, he lived in the state of intense excitement of the leader waiting for the time to charge.

II

The moment was at hand. September had waned, the nights were cooling, his parishioners were returning from the East. One of these was Eleanor Goodrich, whom he met on a corner, tanned and revived from her long summer in Massachusetts. She had inherited the kindly shrewdness of glance characteristic of gentlefolk, the glance that seeks to penetrate externals in its concern for the well-being of those whom it scrutinizes. And he was subtly aware, though she greeted him cordially, that she felt a change in him without being able to account for it.

"I hear you have been here all summer," she said reproachfully. "Mother and father and all of us were much disappointed that you did not come to us on the Cape."

"I should have come, if it had been possible," he replied. "It seems to have done you a world of good."

"Oh, I!" She seemed slightly embarrassed, puzzled, and did not look at him. "I am burned as disgracefully as Evelyn. Phil came on for a month.

"He tells me he hasn't seen you, but that isn't surprising, for he hasn't been to church since June - and he's a vestryman now, too."

She was in mourning for her father-in-law, who had died in the spring. Phil Goodrich had taken his place. Eleanor found the conversation, somehow, drifting out of her control. It was not at all what she would have desired to say. Her colour heightened.

"I have not been conducting the services, but I resume them next Sunday," said the rector. "I ought to tell you," he went on, regarding her, "in view of the conversation we have had, that I have changed my mind concerning a great many things we have talked about - although I have not spoken of this as yet to any of the members of the congregation."

She was speechless, and could only stare at him blankly.

"I mean," he continued, with a calmness that astonished her afterwards, "that I have changed my whole conception as to the functions and future of the Church, that I have come to your position, that we must make up our minds for ourselves, and not have them made up for us. And that we must examine into the truth of all statements, and be governed accordingly."

Her attitude was one of mingled admiration, concern, and awe. And he saw that she had grasped something of the complications which his course was likely to bring about.

"But you are not going to leave us!" she managed to exclaim.

"Not if it is possible to remain," he said, smiling.

"I am so glad." She was still overpowered by the disclosure. "It is good of you to tell me. Do you mind my telling Phil?"

"Not at all," he assured her.

"Will you forgive me," she asked, after a slight pause during which she had somewhat regained her composure, "if I say that I always thought, or rather hoped you would change? that your former beliefs seemed so - unlike you?"

He continued to smile at her as she stepped forward to take the car.

"I'll have to forgive you," he answered, "because you were right - "

She was still in such a state of excitement when she arrived down town that she went direct to her husband's law office.

"I like this!" he exclaimed, as, unannounced, she opened the door of his sanctuary. "You might have caught me with one of those good-looking clients of mine."

Oh, Phil!" she cried, "I've got such a piece of news, I couldn't resist coming to tell you. I met Mr. Hodder - and he's changed."

"Changed!" Phil repeated, looking up at her flushed face beside him. Instead of a law-book, he flung down a time table in which he had been investigating the trains to a quail shooting club in the southern part of the state: The transition to Mr. Hodder was, therefore, somewhat abrupt. "Why, Nell, to look at you, I thought it could be nothing else than my somewhat belated appointment to the United States Supreme Court. How has Hodder changed? I always thought him pretty decent."

"Don't laugh at me," she begged, "it's really serious - and no one knows it yet. He said I might tell you. Do you remember that talk we had at father's, when he first came, and we likened him to a modern Savonarola?"

"And George Bridges took the floor, and shocked mother and Lucy and Laureston," supplied Phil.

"I don't believe mother really was as much shocked as she appeared to be," said Eleanor. "At any rate, the thing that had struck us - you and me - was that Mr. Hodder looked as though he could say something helpful, if he only would. And then I went to see him afterwards, in the parish house - you remember? - after we had been reading modern criticism together, and he told me that the faith which had come down from the fathers was like an egg? It couldn't be chipped. I was awfully disappointed - and yet I couldn't help liking him, he was so honest. And the theological books he gave me to read - which were so mediaeval and absurd! Well, he has come around to our point of view. He told me so himself."

"But what is our point of view, Nell?" her husband asked, with a smile. "Isn't it a good deal like Professor Bridges', only we're not quite so learned? We're just ordinary heathens, as far as I can make out. If Hodder has our point of view, he ought to go into the law or a trust company."

"Oh, Phil!" she protested, "and you're on the vestry! I do believe in Something, and so do you."

"Something," he observed, "is hardly a concrete and complete theology."

"Why do you make me laugh," she reproached him, "when the matter is so serious? What I'm trying to tell you is that I'm sure Mr. Hodder has worked it out. He's too sincere to remain in the Church and not have something constructive and satisfying. I've always said that he seemed to have a truth shut up inside of him which he could not communicate. Well, now he looks as though he were about to communicate it, as though he had discovered it. I suppose you think me silly, but you'll grant, whatever Mr. Hodder may be, he isn't silly. And women can feel these things. You know I'm not given to sentimentality, but I was never so impressed by the growth in any personality as I was this morning by his. He seems to have become himself, as I always imagined him. And, Phil, he was so fine! He's absolutely incapable of posing, as you'll admit, and he stood right up and acknowledged that he'd been wrong in our argument. He hasn't had the services all summer, and when he resumes them next Sunday I gathered that he intends to make his new position clear."

Mr. Goodrich thrust his hands in his pockets and gave a low whistle.

"I guess I won't go shooting Saturday, after all," he declared. "I wouldn't miss Hodder's sermon for all the quail in Harrington County."

"It's high time you did go to church," remarked Eleanor, contemplating, not without pride, her husband's close-cropped, pugnacious head.

Your judgments are pretty sound, Nell. I'll do you that credit. And I've always owned up that Hodder would be a fighter if he ever got started. It's written all over him. What's more, I've a notion that some of our friends are already a little suspicious of him."

"You mean Mr. Parr?" she asked, anxiously.

"No, Wallis Plimpton."

"Oh!" she exclaimed, with disdain in her voice.

"Mr. Parr only got back yesterday, and Wallis told me that Hodder had refused to go on a yachting trip with him. Not only foolishness, but high treason." Phil smiled. "Plimpton's the weather-vane, the barometer of that crowd - he feels a disturbance long before it turns up - he's as sensitive as the stock market."

"He is the stock market," said Eleanor.

"It's been my opinion," Phil went on reflectively, "that they've all had just a trace of uneasiness about Hodder all along, an idea that Nelson Langmaid slipped up for the first time in his life when he got him to come. Oh, the feeling's been dormant, but it existed. And they've been just a little afraid that they couldn't handle him if the time ever came. He's not their type. When I saw Plimpton at the Country Club the other day he wondered, in that genial, off-hand manner of his, whether Hodder would continue to be satisfied with St. John's. Plimpton said he might be offered a missionary diocese. Oh we'll have a fine old row."

"I believe," said Eleanor, "that that's the only thing that interests you."

"Well, it does please me," he admitted, when I think of Gordon Atterbury and Everett Constable and a few others, - Eldon Parr, - who believe that religion ought to be kept archaic and innocuous, served in a form that won't bother anybody. By the way, Nell, do you remember the verse the Professor quoted about the Pharisees, and cleansing the outside of the cup and platter?"

"Yes," she answered, "why?"

"Well - Hodder didn't give you any intimation as to what he intended to do about that sort of thing, did he?"

"What sort of thing?"

"About the inside of Eldon Parr's cup, - so to speak. And the inside of Wallis Plimpton's cup, and Everett Constable's cup, and Ferguson's cup, and Langmaid's. Did it ever strike you that, in St. John's, we have the sublime spectacle of Eldon Parr, the Pharisee in chief, conducting the Church of Christ, who, uttered that denunciation? That's what George Bridges meant. There's something rather ironical in such a situation, to say the least."

"I see," said Eleanor, thoughtfully.

"And what's more, it's typical," continued Phil, energetically, "the big Baptist church on the Boulevard is run by old Sedges, as canny a rascal as you could find in the state. The inside of has cup has never been touched, though he was once immersed in the Mississippi, they say, and swallowed a lot of water."

"Oh, Phil!"

"Hodder's been pretty intimate with Eldon Parr - that always puzzled me," Phil went on. "And yet I'm like you, I never doubted Hodder's honesty. I've always been curious to know what would happen when he found out the kind of thing Eldon Parr is doing every day in his life, making people stand and deliver in the interest of what he would call National Prosperity. Why, that fellow, Funk, they sent to the penitentiary the other day for breaking into the Addicks' house isn't a circumstance to Eldon Parr. He's robbed his tens of thousands, and goes on robbing them right along. By the way, Mr. Parr took most of Addicks' money before Funk got his silver."

"Phil, you have such a ridiculous way of putting things! But I suppose it's true."

"True! I should say it was! There was Mr. Bentley - that was mild. And there never was a hold-up of a western express that could compare to the Consolidated Tractions. Some of these big fellows have the same kind of brain as the professional thieves. Well, they are professional thieves - what's the use of mincing matters! They never try the same game twice. Mr. Parr's getting ready to make another big haul right now. I know, because Plimpton said as much, although he didn't confide in me what this particular piece of rascality is. He knows better." Phil Goodrich looked grim.

"But the law?" exclaimed his wife.

"There never was a law that Nelson Langmaid couldn't drive a horse and carriage through."

"And Mr. Langmaid's one of the nicest men I know!"

"What I wonder," mused Phil, "is whether this is a mere doctrinal revolt on Hodder's part, or whether he has found out a few things. There are so many parsons in these days who don't seem to see any inconsistency in robbing several thousand people to build settlement houses and carved marble altars, and who wouldn't accept a Christmas box from a highwayman. But I'll do Hodder the justice to say he doesn't strike me as that kind. And I have an idea that Eldon Parr and Wallis Plimpton and the rest know he isn't, know that he'd be a Tartar if he ever get started, and that's what makes them uneasy."

"Then it isn't his change of religious opinions they would care about?" said Eleanor.

"Oh, I don't say that Eldon Parr won't try to throw him out if he questions the faith as delivered by the Saints."

"Phil, what a way of putting it!"

"Any indication of independence, any approach to truth would be regarded as dangerous," Phil continued. And of course Gordon Atterbury and others we could mention, who think they believe in the unchipped egg theory, will be outraged. But it's deeper than that. Eldon Parr will give orders that Hodder's to go."

"Give orders?"

"Certainly. That vestry, so far as Mr. Parr is concerned, is a mere dummy board of directors. He's made Langmaid, and Plimpton, and even Everett Constable, who's the son of an honourable gentleman, and ought to know better. And he can ruin them by snapping his fingers. He can even make the financial world too hot for Ferguson. I'll say this for Gordon Atterbury, that Mr. Parr can't control him, but he's got a majority without him, and Gordon won't vote for a heretic. Who are left, except father-in-law Waring and myself?"

"He can't control either of you!" said Eleanor, proudly.

"When it comes to that, Nell - we'll move into Canada and buy a farm."

"But can he hurt you, Phil - either of you?" she asked, after a moment.

"I'd like to see him try it," Phil Goodrich declared

And his wife thought, as she looked at him, that she would like to see Mr. Parr try it, too.

III

Phil Goodrich had once said that Mr. Plimpton's translation of the national motto E pluribus unum, was "get together," and it was true that not the least of Mr. Plimpton's many gifts was that of peace making. Such was his genius that he scented trouble before it became manifest to the world, and he stoutly declared that no difference of opinion ever existed between reasonable men that might not be patched up before the breach became too wide - provided that a third reasonable man contributed his services. The qualifying word "reasonable" is to be noted. When Mr. Bedloe Hubbell had undertaken, in the name of Reform, to make a witch's cauldron of the city's politics, which Mr. Beatty had hitherto conducted so smoothly from the back room of his saloon, Mr. Plimpton had unselfishly offered his services. Bedloe Hubbell, although he had been a playmate of Mr. Plimpton's wife's, had not proved "reasonable," and had rejected with a scorn only to be deemed fanatical the suggestion that Mr. Hubbell's interests and Mr. Beatty's interests need not clash, since Mr. Hubbell might go to Congress! And Mr. Plimpton was the more hurt since the happy suggestion was his own, and he had had no little difficulty in getting Mr. Beatty to agree to it.

Yet Mr. Plimpton's career in the ennobling role of peacemaker had, on the whole, been crowned with such success as to warrant his belief in the principle. Mr. Parr, for instance, - in whose service, as in that of any other friend, Mr. Plimpton was always ready to act - had had misunderstandings with eminent financiers, and sometimes with United States Senators. Mr.

Plimpton had made many trips to the Capitol at Washington, sometimes in company with Mr. Langmaid, sometimes not, and on one memorable occasion had come away smiling from an interview with the occupant of the White House himself.

Lest Mr. Plimpton's powers of premonition seem supernatural, it may be well to reveal the comparative simplicity of his methods. Genius, analyzed, is often disappointing, Mr. Plimpton's was selective and synthetic. To illustrate in a particular case, he had met Mr. Parr in New York and had learned that the Reverend Mr. Hodder had not only declined to accompany the banker on a yachting trip, but had elected to remain in the city all summer, in his rooms in the parish house, while conducting no services. Mr. Parr had thought this peculiar. On his return home Mr. Plimpton had one day dropped in to see a Mr. Gaines, the real estate agent for some of his property. And Mr. Plimpton being hale-fellow-well-met, Mr. Gaines had warned him jestingly that he would better not let his parson know that he owned a half interest in a certain hotel in Dalton Street, which was leased at a profitable rate.

If Mr. Plimpton felt any uneasiness, he did not betray it. And he managed to elicit from the agent, in an entirely casual and jovial manner, the fact that Mr. Hodder, a month or so before, had settled the rent of a woman for a Dalton Street flat, and had been curious to discover the name of the owner. Mr. Gaines, whose business it was to recognize everybody, was sure of Mr. Hodder, although he had not worn clerical clothes.

Mr. Plimpton became very thoughtful when he had left the office. He visited Nelson Langmaid in the Parr

Building. And the result of the conference was to cause Mr. Langmaid to recall, with a twinge of uneasiness, a certain autumn morning in a room beside Bremerton Lake when he had been faintly yet distinctly conscious of the, admonitory whisperings of that sixth sense which had saved him on other occasions.

"Dash it!" he said to himself, after Mr. Plimpton had departed, and he stood in the window and gazed across at the flag on the roof of 'Ferguson's.' "It would serve me right for meddling in this parson business. Why did I take him away from Jerry Whitely, anyhow?"

It added to Nelson Langmaid's discomfort that he had a genuine affection, even an admiration for the parson in question. He might have known by looking at the man that he would wake up some day, - such was the burden of his lament. And there came to him, ironically out of the past, the very words of Mr. Parr's speech to the vestry after Dr. Gilman's death, that succinct list of qualifications for a new rector which he himself, Nelson Langmaid, had humorously and even more succinctly epitomized. Their "responsibility to the parish, to the city, and to God" had been to find a rector "neither too old nor too young, who would preach the faith as we received it, who was not sensational, and who did not mistake Socialism for Christianity." At the "Socialism" a certain sickly feeling possessed the lawyer, and he wiped beads of perspiration from his dome-like forehead.

He didn't pretend to be versed in theology - so he had declared - and at the memory of these words of his the epithet "ass," self applied, passed his lips. "You want a parson who will stick to his last, not too high or too low or too broad or too narrow, who has intellect without too much initiative . . . and will not get the church uncomfortably full of strangers and run you out of your pews." Thus he had capped the financier. Well, if they had caught a tartar, it served him, Nelson Langmaid, right. He recalled his talk with Gerald Whitely, and how his brother-in-law had lost his temper when they had got on the subject of personality . . . .

Perhaps Wallis Plimpton could do something. Langmaid's hopes of this were not high. It may have been that he had suspicions of what Mr. Plimpton would have called Hodder's "reasonableness." One thing was clear - that Mr. Plimpton was frightened. In the sanctuaries, the private confessionals of high finance (and Nelson Langmaid's office may be called so), the more primitive emotions are sometimes exhibited.

"I don't see what business it is of a clergyman, or of any one else, whether I own property in Dalton Street," Mr. Plimpton had said, as he sat on the edge of the lawyer's polished mahogany desk. "What does he expect us to do, - allow our real estate to remain unproductive merely for sentimental reasons? That's like a parson, most of 'em haven't got any more common sense than that. What right has he got to go nosing around Dalton Street? Why doesn't he stick to his church?"

"I thought you fellows were to build him a settlement house there," Langmaid observed.

"On the condition that he wouldn't turn socialist."

"You'd better have stipulated it in the bond," said the

lawyer, who could not refrain, even at this solemn moment, from the temptation of playingupon Mr. Plimpton's apprehensions. "I'm afraid he'll make it his business, Wallis, to find out whether you own anything in Dalton Street. I'll bet he's got a list of Dalton Street property in his pocket right now."

Mr. Plimpton groaned.

"Thank God I don't own any of it!" said Langmaid.

"What the deuce does he intend to do?" the other demanded.

"Read it out in church," Langmaid suggested. "It wouldn't sound pretty, Wallis, to be advertised in the post on Monday morning as owning that kind of a hotel."

"Oh, he's a gentleman," said Mr. Plimpton, "he wouldn't do anything as low as that!"

"But if he's become a socialist?" objected Langmaid.

"He wouldn't do it," his friend reiterated, none too confidently. "I shouldn't be surprised if he made me resign from the vestry and forced me to sell my interest. It nets me five thousand a year."

"What is the place?" Langmaid asked sympathetically, "Harrod's?"

Mr. Plimpton nodded.

"Not that I am a patron," the lawyer explained somewhat hastily. "But I've seen the building, going home."

"It looks to me as if it would burn down some day, Wallis."

"I wish it would," said Mr. Plimpton.

"If it's any comfort to you - to us," Langmaid went on, after a moment, "Eldon Parr owns the whole block above Thirteenth, on the south side - bought it three years ago. He thinks the business section will grow that way."

"I know," said Mr. Plimpton, and they looked at each other.

The name predominant in both minds had been mentioned.

"I wonder if Hodder really knows what he's up against." Mr. Plimpton sometimes took refuge in slang.

"Well, after all, we're not sure yet that he's "up against anything," replied Langmaid, who thought the time had come for comfort. "It may all be a false alarm. There's no reason, after all, why a Christian clergyman shouldn't rescue women in Dalton Street, and remain in the city to study the conditions of the neighbourhood where his settlement house is to be. And just, because you or I would not be able to resist an invitation to go yachting with Eldon Parr, a man might be imagined who had that amount of moral courage."

"That's just it. Hodder seems to me, now I come to think of it, just the kind of John Brown type who wouldn't hesitate to get into a row with Eldon Parr if he thought it was right, and pull down any amount of disagreeable stuff about our ears."

"You're mixing your heroes, Wallis," said Langmaid.

"I can't help it. You'd catch it, too, Nelson. What in the name of sense possessed you to get such a man?"

This being a question the lawyer was unable to answer, the conversation came to another pause. And it was then that Mr. Plimpton's natural optimism reasserted itself.

"It isn't done, - the thing we're afraid of, that's all," he proclaimed, after a turn or two about the room. "Hodder's a gentleman, as I said, and if he feels as we suspect he does he'll resign like a gentleman and a Christian. I'll have a talk with him - oh, you can trust me! I've got an idea. Gordon Atterbury told me the other day there is a vacancy in a missionary diocese out west, and that Hodder's name had been mentioned, among others, to the bishops for the place. He'd make a rattling missionary bishop, you know, holding services in saloons and knocking men's heads together for profanity, and he boxes like a professional. Now, a word from Eldon Parr might turn the trick. Every parson wants to be a bishop."

Langmaid shook his head.

"You're getting out of your depths, my friend. The Church isn't Wall Street. And missionary bishops aren't chosen to make convenient vacancies."

"I don't mean anything crude," Mr. Plimpton protested. "But a word from the chief layman of a diocese like this, a man who never misses a General Convention, and does everything handsomely, might count, - particularly if they're already thinking of Hodder. The bishops would never suspect we wanted to get rid of him."

"Well," said Langmaid, "I advise you to go easy, all along the line."

"Oh, I'll go easy enough," Mr. Plimpton assented, smiling. "Do you remember how I pulled off old Senator Matthews when everybody swore he was dead set on voting for an investigation in the matter of those coal lands Mr. Parr got hold of in his state?"

"Matthews isn't Hodder, by a long shat," said Langmaid. "If you ask me my opinion, I'll tell you frankly that if Hodder has made up his mind to stay in St. John's a ton of dynamite and all the Eldon Parrs in the nation can't get him out,"

"Can't the vestry make him resign?" asked Mr. Plimpton, uncomfortably.

"You'd better, go home and study your canons, my friend. Nothing short of conviction for heresy can do it, if he doesn't want to go."

"You wouldn't exactly call him a heretic," Mr. Plimpton said ruefully.

"Would you know a heretic if you saw one?" demanded Langmaid.

"No, but my wife would, and Gordon Atterbury and Constable would, and Eldon Parr. But don't let's get nervous."

"Well, that's sensible at any rate," said Langmaid . . . .

So Mr. Plimpton had gone off optimistic, and felt even more so the next morning after he had had his breakfast in the pleasant dining room of the Gore Mansion, of which he was now master. As he looked out through the open window at the sunshine in the foliage of Waverley Place, the prospect of his being removed from that position of dignity and influence on the vestry of St. John's, which he had achieved, with others, after so much walking around the walls, seemed remote. And he reflected with satisfaction upon the fact that his wife, who was his prime minister, would be home from the East that day. Two heads were better than one, especially if one of the two were Charlotte Gore's. And Mr. Plimpton had often reflected upon the loss to the world, and the gain to himself, that she was a woman.

It would not be gallant to suggest that his swans were geese.

IV

The successful navigation of lower Tower Street, at noonday, required presence of mind on the part of the pedestrian. There were currents and counter-currents, eddies and backwaters, and at the corner of Vine a veritable maelstrom through which two lines of electric cars pushed their way, east and weft, north and south, with incessant clanging of bells; followed by automobiles with resounding horns, trucks and delivery wagons with wheels reverberating on the granite. A giant Irish policeman, who seemed in continual danger of a violent death, and wholly indifferent to it, stood between the car tracks and halted the rush from time to time, driving the people like sheep from one side to the other. Through the doors of Ferguson's poured two conflicting streams of humanity, and wistful groups of young women, on the way from hasty lunches, blocked the pavements and stared at the finery behind the plate-glass windows.

The rector, slowly making his way westward, permitted himself to be thrust hither and thither, halted and shoved on again as he studied the faces of the throng. And presently he found himself pocketed before one of the exhibits of feminine interest, momentarily helpless, listening to the admiring and envious chorus of a bevy of diminutive shop-girls on the merits of a Paris gown. It was at this moment that he perceived, pushing towards him with an air of rescue, the figure of his vestryman, Mr. Wallis Plimpton.

"Well, well, well!" he cried, as he seized Hodder by

the arm and pulled him towards the curb. "What are you doing herein the marts of trade? Come right along with me to the Eyrie, and we'll have something, to eat."

The Eyrie was a famous lunch club, of limited membership, at the top of the Parr Building, where financial affairs of the first importance were discussed and settled.

Hodder explained that he had lunched at half-past twelve.

"Well, step into my office a minute. It does me good, to see you again, upon my word, and I can't let you get by without a little pow-wow."

Mr. Plimpton's trust company, in Vine Street, resembled a Greek temple. Massive but graceful granite columns adorned its front, while within it was partitioned off with polished marble and ornamental grills. In the rear, guarded by the desks and flanked by the compartments of various subordinates, was the president's private sanctum, and into this holy of holies Mr. Plimpton led the way with the simple, unassuming genial air of the high priest of modern finance who understands men. The room was eloquent almost to affectation of the system and order of great business, inasmuch as it betrayed not the least sign of a workshop. On the dark oak desk were two leather-bound books and a polished telephone. The walls were panelled, there was a stone fireplace with andirons set, a deep carpet spread over the tessellated floor, and three leather-padded armchairs, one of which Mr. Plimpton hospitably drew forward for the rector. He then produced a box of cigars.

"You don't smoke, Mr. Hodder. I always forget. That's the way you manage to keep yourself in such good shape." He drew out a gold match box and seated himself with an air of gusto opposite his guest. "And you haven't had a vacation, they tell me."

"On the contrary," said the rector, "McCrae has taken the services all summer."

"But you've been in the city!" Mr. Plimpton exclaimed, puffing at his cigar.

"Yes, I've been in the city."

"Well, well, I'll bet you haven't been idle. Just between us, as friends, Mr. Hodder, I've often wondered if you didn't work too hard - there's such a thing as being too conscientious, you know. And I've an idea that the rest of the vestry think so. Mr. Parr, for instance. We know when we've got a good thing, and we don't want to wear you out. Oh, we can appreciate your point of view, and admire it. But a little relaxation - eh? It's too bad that you couldn't have seen your way to take that cruise - Mr. Parr was all cut up about it. I guess you're the only man among all of us fairly close to him, who really knows him well," said Mr. Plimpton, admiringly. "He thinks a great deal of you, Mr. Hodder. By the way, have you seen him since he got back?"

No," Hodder answered."

"The trip did him good. I thought he was a little seedy in the spring - didn't you? Wonderful man! And when I think how he's slandered and abused it makes me hot.

And he never says anything, never complains, lives up there all alone, and takes his medicine. That's real patriotism, according to my view. He could retire to-morrow - but he keeps on - why? Because he feels the weight of a tremendous responsibility on his shoulders, because he knows if it weren't for him and men like him upon whom the prosperity of this nation depends, we'd have famine and anarchy on our hands in no time. And look what he's done for the city, without ostentation, mind you! He never blows his own horn-never makes a speech. And for the Church! But I needn't tell you. When this settlement house and chapel are finished, they'll be coming out here from New York to get points. By the way, I meant to have written you. Have our revised plans come yet? We ought to break ground in November, oughtn't we?"

"I intend to lay my views on that matter before the vestry at the next meeting, the rector said.

"Well," declared Mr. Plimpton, after a scarcely perceptible pause, "I've no doubt they'll be worth listening to. If I were to make a guess," he continued, with a contemplative smile, blowing a thin stream of smoke towards the distant ceiling, "I should bet that you have spent your summer looking over the ground. I don't say that you have missed your vocation, Mr. Hodder, but I don't mind telling you that for a clergyman, for a man absorbed in spiritual matters, a man who can preach the sermons you preach, you've got more common-sense and business thoroughness than any one I have ever run across in your profession."

"Looking over the ground?" Hodder repeated, ignoring the compliment.

"Sure, said Mr. Plimpton, smiling more benignly than ever. "You mustn't be modest about it. Dalton Street. And when that settlement house is built, I'll guarantee it will be run on a business basis. No nonsense."

"What do you mean by nonsense?" Hodder asked. He did not make the question abrupt, and there was even the hint of a smile in his eyes, which Mr. Plimpton found the more disquieting.

"Why, that's only a form of speech. I mean you'll be practical, efficient, that you'll get hold of the people of that neighbourhood and make 'em see that the world isn't such a bad place after all, make 'em realize that we in St. John's want to help 'em out. That you won't make them more foolishly discontented than they are, and go preaching socialism to them."

"I have no intention of preaching socialism," said Hodder. But he laid a slight emphasis on the word which sent a cold shiver down Mr. Plimpton's spine, and made him wonder whether there might not be something worse than socialism.

"I knew you wouldn't," he declared, with all the heartiness he could throw into his voice. "I repeat, you're a practical, sensible man. I'll yield to none in my belief in the Church as a moral, uplifting, necessary spiritual force in our civilization, in my recognition of her high ideals, but we business men, Mr. Hodder, - as - I am sure you must agree, - have got to live, I am sorry to say, on a lower plane. We've got to deal with the world as we find it, and do our little best to help things along. We can't take the Gospel literally, or we should all be ruined in a day, and swamp everybody else. You understand me?

"I understand you," said the rector.

Mr. Plimpton's cigar had gone out. In spite of himself, he had slipped from the easy-going, casual tone into one that was becoming persuasive, apologetic, strenuous. Although the day was not particularly warm, he began to perspire a little; and he repeated the words over to himself, "I understand you." What the deuce did the rector know? He had somehow the air of knowing everything - more than Mr. Plimpton did. And Mr. Plimpton was beginning to have the unusual and most disagreeable feeling of having been weighed in the balance and found wanting. He glanced at his guest, who sat quite still, the head bent a trifle, the disturbing gray eyes fixed contemplatively an him - accusingly. And yet the accusation did not seem personal with the clergyman, whose eyes were nearly the medium, the channels of a greater, an impersonal Ice. It was true that the man had changed. He was wholly baffling to Mr. Plimpton, whose sense of alarm increased momentarily into an almost panicky feeling as he remembered what Langmaid had said. Was this inscrutable rector of St. John's gazing, knowingly, at the half owner of Harrods Hotel in Dalton Street, who couldn't take the Gospel literally? There was evidently no way to find out at once, and suspense would be unbearable, in vain he told himself that these thoughts were nonsense, the discomfort persisted, and he had visions of that career in which he had become one of the first citizens and the respected husband of Charlotte Gore clashing down about his ears. Why? Because a clergyman should choose to be quixotic, fanatical? He did not took quixotic, fanatical, Mr. Plimpton had to admit, - but a good deal saner than he, Mr. Plimpton, must have appeared at that moment. His throat was dry, and he didn't dare to make the attempt to relight his cigar.

"There's nothing like getting together - keeping in touch with people, Mr. Hodder," he managed to say. "I've been out of town a good deal this summer - putting on a little flesh, I'm sorry to admit. But I've been meaning to drop into the parish house and talk over those revised plans with you. I will drop in - in a day or two. I'm interested in the work, intensely interested, and so is Mrs. Plimpton. She'll help you. I'm sorry you can't lunch with me."

He had the air, now, of the man who finds himself disagreeably and unexpectedly closeted. with a lunatic; and his language, although he sought to control it, became eves a trifle less coherent.

"You must make allowances for us business men, Mr. Hodder. I mean, of course, we're sometimes a little lax in our duties - in the summer, that is. Don't shoot the pianist, he's doing his - ahem! You know the story.

"By the way, I hear great things of you; I'm told it's on the cards that you're to be made a bishop."

"Oh," answered the rector, "there are better men mentioned than I!"

"I want you to know this," said his vestryman, as he seized Hodder's hand, "much as we value you here, bitterly as we should hate to lose you, none of us, I am sure, would stand in the way of such a deserved advancement."

"Thank you, Mr. Plimpton," said the rector.

Mr. Plimpton watched the vigorous form striding through the great chamber until it disappeared. Then he seized his hat and made his way as rapidly as possible through the crowds to the Parr Building. At the entrance of the open-air roof garden of the Eyrie he ran into Nelson Langmaid.

"You're the very man I'm after," said Mr. Plimpton, breathlessly. "I stopped in your office, and they said you'd gone up."

"What's the matter, Wallis?" inquired the lawyer, tranquilly. "You look as if you'd lost a couple of bonds."

I've just seen Hodder, and he is going to do it."

"Do what?"

"Sit down here, at this table in the corner, and I'll tell you."

For a practical man, it must be admitted that Mr. Plimpton had very little of the concrete to relate. And it appeared on cross-examination by Mr. Langmaid, who ate his cold meat and salad with an exasperating and undiminished appetite - that the only definite thing the rector had said was that he didn't intend to preach socialism. This was reassuring.

"Reassuring!" exclaimed Mr. Plimpton, whose customary noonday hunger was lacking, "I wish you could have heard him say it!"

"The wicked," remarked the lawyer, "flee when no man pursueth. Don't shoot the pianist!" Langmaid set down his beer, and threw back his head and laughed. "If I were the Reverend Mr. Hodder, after such an exhibition as you gave, I should immediately have suspected the pianist of something, and I should have gone off by myself and racked my brains and tried to discover what it was. He's a clever man, and if he hasn't got a list of Dalton Street property now he'll have one by to-morrow, and the story of some of your transactions with Tom Beatty and the City Council."

"I believe you'd joke in the electric chair," said Mr. a Plimpton, resentfully. "I'll tell you this, - and my experience backs me up, - if you can't get next to a man by a little plain talk, he isn't safe. I haven't got the market sense for nothing, and I'll give you this tip, Nelson, - it's time to stand from under. Didn't I warn you fellows that Bedloe Hubbell meant business long before he started in? and this parson can give Hubbell cards and spades. Hodder can't see this thing as it is. He's been thinking, this summer. And a man of that kind is downright dangerous when he begins to think. He's found out things, and he's put two and two together, and he's the uncompromising type. He has a notion that the Gospel can be taken literally, and I could feel all the time I was talking to him he thought I was a crook."

"Perhaps he was right," observed the lawyer.

"That comes well from you," Mr. Plimpton retorted.

Oh, I'm a crook, too," said Langmaid. "I discovered it some time ago. The difference between you and me, Wallis, is that I am willing to acknowledge it, and you're not. The whole business world, as we know it, is crooked, and if we don't cut other people's throats, they'll cut ours."

"And if we let go, what would happen to the country?" his companion demanded.

Langmaid began to shake with silent laughter.

"Your solicitude about the country, Wallis, is touching. I was brought up to believe that patriotism had an element of sacrifice in it, but I can't see ours. And I can't imagine myself, somehow, as a Hercules bearing the burden of our Constitution. From Mr. Hodder's point of view, perhaps, - and I'm not sure it isn't the right one, the pianist is doing his damnedest, to the tune of - Dalton Street. We might as well look this thing in the face, my friend. You and I really don't believe in another world, or we shouldn't be taking so much trouble to make this one as we'd like to have it."

"I never expected to hear you talk this way," said Mr. Plimpton.

"Well, it's somewhat of a surprise to me," the lawyer admitted.

"And I don't think you put it fairly," his friend contended. "I never can tell when you are serious, but this is damned serious. In business we have to deal with crooks, who hold us up right and left, and if we stood back you know as well as I do that everything would go to pot. And if we let the reformers have their way the country would be bedlam. We'd have anarchy and bloodshed, revolution, and the people would be calling us, the strong men, back in no time. You can't change human nature. And we have a sense of responsibility - we support law and order and the

Church, and found institutions, and give millions away in charity."

The big lawyer listened to this somewhat fervent defence of his order with an amused smile, nodding his head slightly from side to side.

"If you don't believe in it," demanded Mr. Plimpton, why the deuce don't you drop it?"

"It's because of my loyalty," said Langmaid. "I wouldn't desert my pals. I couldn't bear, Wallis, to see you go to the guillotine without me."

Mr. Plimpton became unpleasantly silent.

"Well, you may think it's a joke," he resumed, after a moment, "but there will be a guillotine if we don't look out. That confounded parson is getting ready to spring something, and I'm going to give Mr. Parr a tip. He'll know how to handle him. He doesn't talk much, but I've got an idea, from one or two things he let drop, that he's a little suspicious of a change in Hodder. But he ought to be waived."

"You're in no condition to talk to Mr. Parr, or to anyone else, except your wife, Walks," Langmaid said. "You'd better go home, and let me see Mr. Parr. I'm responsible for Mr. Hodder, anyway."

"All right," Mr. Plimpton agreed, as though he had gained some shred of comfort from this thought. "I guess you're in worse than any of us."

Notes

Notes

Notes

H. Irving Hancock
H. Rider Haggard
H. W. C. Davis
Hamilton Wright Mabie
Hans Christian Andersen
Harold Avery
Harold McGrath
Harriet Beecher Stowe
Harry Houidini
Helent Hunt Jackson
Helen Nicolay
Hendrik Conscience
Hendy David Thoreau
Henri Barbusse
Henrik Ibsen
Henry Adams
Henry Ford
Henry Frost
Henry James
Henry Jones Ford
Henry Seton Merriman
Henry W Longfellow
Herbert A. Giles
Herbert N. Casson
Herman Hesse
Homer
Honore De Balzac
Horace Walpole
Horatio Alger Jr.
Howard Pyle
Howard R. Garis
Hugh Lofting
Hugh Walpole
Humphry Ward
Ian Maclaren
Inez Haynes Gillmore
Irving Bacheller
Israel Abrahams
Ivan Turgenev
J.G.Austin
J. Henri Fabre
J. M. Barrie
J. Macdonald Oxley
J. S. Fletcher
J. S. Knowles
J. Storer Clouston
Jack London
Jacob Abbott
James Allen
James Andrews
James Baldwin
James DeMille
James Joyce
James Lane Allen
James Lane Allen
James Oliver Curwood
James Oppenheim
James Otis
James R. Driscoll
Jane Austen
Jens Peter Jacobsen
Jerome K. Jerome
John Burroughs
John Cournos
John F. Kennedy
John Gay
John Glasworthy
John Habberton
John Joy Bell
John Kendrick Bangs
John Milton
John Philip Sousa
Jonas Lauritz Idemil Lie
Jonathan Swift
Joseph A. Altsheler
Joseph Carey
Joseph Conrad
Joseph E. Badger Jr
Joseph Hergesheimer
Joseph Jacobs
Julian Hawthrone
Julies Vernes
Justin Huntly McCarthy
Kakuzo Okakura
Kenneth Grahame
Kenneth McGaffey
Kate Langley Bosher
Kate Langley Bosher
Katherine Cecil Thurston
Katherine Stokes
L. A. Abbot
L. T. Meade
L. Frank Baum
Latta Griswold
Laura Lee Hope
Laurence Housman
Leo Tolstoy
Leonid Andreyev
Lewis Carroll
Lilian Bell
Lloyd Osbourne
Louis Tracy
Louisa May Alcott
Lucy Fitch Perkins
Lucy Maud Montgomery
Lydia Miller Middleton
Lyndon Orr
M. Corvus
M. H. Adams
Margaret E. Sangster
Margaret Vandercook
Margret Penrose
Maria Edgeworth
Maria Thompson Daviess
Mariano Azuela
Marion Polk Angellotti
Mark Overton
Mark Twain
Mary Austin
Mary Catherine Crowley
Mary Cole
Mary Hastings Bradley
Mary Roberts Rinehart
Mary Rowlandson
M. Wollstonecraft Shelley
Maud Lindsay
Max Beerbohm
Myra Kelly
Nathaniel Hawthrone
Nicolo Machiavelli
O. F. Walton
Oscar Wilde
Owen Johnson
P.G. Wodehouse
Paul and Mabel Thorne
Paul G. Tomlinson
Paul Severing
Percy Brebner
Peter B. Kyne
Plato
R. Derby Holmes
R. L. Stevenson
R. S. Ball
Rabindranath Tagore
Rahul Alvares
Ralph Henry Barbour
Ralph Waldo Emmerson
Rene Descartes
Rex Beach
Rex E. Beach
Richard Harding Davis
Richard Jefferies
Richard Le Gallienne

Robert Barr
Robert Frost
Robert Gordon Anderson
Robert L. Drake
Robert Lansing
Robert Lynd
Robert Michael Ballantyne
Robert W. Chambers
Rosa Nouchette Carey
Rudyard Kipling
Samuel B. Allison
Samuel Hopkins Adams
Sarah Bernhardt
Selma Lagerlof
Sherwood Anderson
Sigmund Freud
Standish O'Grady
Stanley Weyman
Stella Benson
Stephen Crane
Stewart Edward White
Stijn Streuvels
Swami Abhedananda
Swami Parmananda
T. S. Ackland
T. S. Arthur
The Princess Der Ling
Thomas A. Janvier
Thomas A Kempis
Thomas Anderton
Thomas Bailey Aldrich
Thomas Bulfinch
Thomas De Quincey
Thomas H. Huxley
Thomas Hardy
Thomas More
Thornton W. Burgess
U. S. Grant
Valentine Williams
Various Authors
Victor Appleton
Virginia Woolf
Walter Camp
Walter Scott
Washington Irving
Wilbur Lawton
Wilkie Collins
Willa Cather
Willard F. Baker
William Dean Howells
William le Queux
W. Makepeace Thackeray
William W. Walter
Winston Churchill
Yei Theodora Ozaki
Yogi Ramacharaka
Young E. Allison
Zane Grey

www.ingramcontent.com/pod-product-compliance
Lightning Source LLC
Chambersburg PA
CBHW020547310726
48979CB00008B/1118/J

* 9 7 8 1 4 2 1 8 0 6 9 3 8 *